BEAR-FACED LIES
& OTHER FICTIONS

short stories

Also by B. Mamatha:

B. Mamatha

Bear-faced Lies
& Other Fictions

The Goldman Press

CONTENTS

Out of Nature

The Bears were running again, roaming the streets in the name of martial law: policing some, devouring others. You never knew which side of the law would find you first.

The rest of us stayed hidden, holed up the suburbs – in towering apartments cut into granite cliff-faces; in buildings that were once schools and churches and pinnacles of everything that was believed to be beautiful. We –

They had been abandoned, left behind by parents who clung instead to that political belief which is always altruistic for the children of others. David and Kesha were still cubs, mewling and rattling in their sagging furs. The grandparents were bed-bound. Ursula was quiet much of the time, watching the sky hanging above the valley, and the river far below. Her face had grown mean-looking: like the rest of them she was slowly starving.

They had been in the apartment for weeks, watching the world on the television set and feeling adrift in the wind. Neighbours died behind their doors, and the hallways grew heavy with the stench of it. It was an invitation that brought others, inquisitive and growling with hunger.

Once someone came to their apartment; a dense-furred fellow, too dusty to be militia. He poked his muzzle past the door and told Ursula he was trying to cut a deal for his family. He was dying, he said; was she interested? He spoke in a low growl, whiskers jumping in the dark, trying to catch the scent of them behind their bed sheets.

"We have no money," Ursula said.

"You're starving. We could come to some arrangement." Unctuous voice, like molasses on dry stone.

"What arrangement? We have nothing. Your family would benefit more if … We have nothing."

"Wait." His claws curled around the side of the door, the chain squealing on its bolts but holding fast.

Through the peephole Ursula saw him drop down onto all fours, shuffling his girth into the gloom. His head moved on his broad neck as he went; shawl of shadows, rolls of fat. His shoulder blades had worked like pistons.

David took to luring birds onto the balcony, and Ursula let him because he was still a cub. She would sit at the dining table smoking while he lay like a pebble against the railings. Eventually some sparrow might come, inquisitive and foolish, and David would spring up. He always missed, and then the cigarette would smoke itself while Ursula raced to the glass door in case he was caught in the breeze and hurled down. A death against the rocks: such a waste.

Meanwhile the river rolled on in empty promise. The Bears had dammed upstream, corralling the last of the fish into neat pens. The weeds grew verdant, but even they were a risk: what the Bears didn't think fit for eating they still patrolled.

The parents had sent letters – at first. Missives from foreign borders about how they'd reached as far as such a place, or tales of the rain-soaked coast, or that there was a resistance, a collective, hope.

"When are they coming home?" Kesha had asked.

Ursula ate the letter. They stopped collecting the mail, or it stopped coming; it was hard to know which.

Kesha with her dark, placid eyes and lean face; always watchful, always coiled in her limbs. While David clawed against the sky and missed, it was Kesha who had reared up from the shadows and made the first kill. It was a marbled bird, a petrel; grey soon mottled with red. Even the grandparents seemed to stir in their room, bedsprings creaking with the agony of intuition. The smell! Like dark rust; like a memory of something lost – heady and delicious and binding.

They fought for it, Ursula and the cubs rolling across the balcony, their bodies pressed strange against the railings. A wing was ripped from the meat of the body and discarded like a fan. Feathers in the air. Thin glaze of blood seeping over the precipice and easing, drop by drop, into the water way below; each one spread and pulled apart by the current and carried away, indistinguishable.

Ursula lashed out with her back legs, kicking lines of captaincy on the cubs' shoulders. The bird was ripped insides out, twined in a scarlet scarf of entrails and ovaries. Ursula pushed her muzzle into the cavity, teeth and tongue fighting for grip, and then the tiny skeleton splintered and fragments of bird flew free into the air. It was little more than a morsel.

The smell of the bird … the smell of the bird. It had lured them all onto their haunches. The petrel's head was alone untouched, a pale ball rolling forlornly against the granite. Ursula left it for the cubs and came inside. For a few moments life in its meanest aspect had flown into the corners of the apartment and clung there like gauze.

It was that day – or the day after, or that week – or one that followed, when Ursula said they needed to find food.

The cubs looked at each other blankly. Already the notion of fending for themselves was a thin smear beneath lethargy.

"But how?"

Ursula trembled inside herself. "I'll go to the mall."

She walked to the kitchen, tottering on hind legs between the chairs and the roses woven into the carpet. They kept a small tin on an upper shelf; a long time ago the father had stuffed it full of money – curls of paper notes and loose, rattling coins.

"But." David sat hunched over a plastic spinner. He jerked the handle petulantly and it sprang across the carpet and toppled over.

Ursula shook the tin. A few coins rolled into her palm and she tucked them into the pocket of her cotton bag.

"I'm light on my feet. I'm wily." She turned at the door and grinned in such a way that all her teeth were bared, all at once.

"I'll be back soon," she sang, voice like gravel; like the lie in their bellies.

She took the long way, cutting through the suburbs and the quiet, sleeping streets. She climbed the hill and watched the tower blocks reaching for the clouds in surrender. Hollow bollards, their insides lay sprawled around in a blast radius: sofas and wardrobe doors; bed legs fractured from their spines; sheets mounded like corpses. Gutted buildings framed others, empty and stacked face-to-face, like dominoes devoid of spots. On one floor – eight stories up and hooked on its last surviving corner – a bicycle rested against a bathtub.

She passed a playground, the rubber matting scorched with petrol lines. The swings rocked in the wind, plastic seats melted into teary faces that squealed on rusted hinges, a see-saw melody of no good. In the hollowed ground beneath, a yellow parcel lay waiting to be unwrapped.

The melody played through the grass; the grass danced in time. Ursula sniffed: the breeze blew acrid and bereft. She drew level with the swings and the wind flipped the covers of the little yellow lump and she saw then that it had been a dog, once. A collar was welded to the remains of its throat; fragments of skin slick and shining as after rain. Mostly it was bone, washed clean, eyeballs staring out on the world. Once it had been someone's pet, and now it too was gutted and hollow.

She circled warily, surveying the fallen landscape. Trees crippled in their roots. Clouds nudging the horizon with their skirts in their hands. Nothing to salvage, and the morning growing lean while, somewhere in the distance, pebbles jumped against the broken road and were silenced.

Ursula moved quickly, striding along the brow of the hill and ducking between the tree bones. The grass sprang over her footsteps, unmarked but for the cradle of her scent.

Garvin was a different world; it was moneyed. Its mall was a concrete labyrinth: folds of underground tunnels crested with tiny mosaic squares and fleurs-de-lis. And bustling! So busy, with a great clamouring, it seemed, to buy or berate, or just to mark the moment of being with noise. There were bears in second furs and winter coats. Some had animal skins draped over a shoulder, or were knotted in silk ties and scarves, while their eyes never stopped darting this way and that.

It was a fool's errand; an unfamiliar landscape where nothing could be bought for the money she had. The cheapest shops were in the guts of the building, far underground. Ursula followed the crowd, all of them streaming downhill, tap, tap, tapping against the tiles and the noise growing to a great tumult of applause. Stifled lights bounced against the store fronts, glassy-eyed reflections observing how they packed themselves together.

A commotion had broken out somewhere at the back – a high female voice snarling purple indignation and belly roars. Ursula slowed to look, and the weight of the crowd tipped and pinned her against a jeweller's shop: gleam of gold against her back, and bodies all around.

The angry voice skated overhead and was lost. Ursula tried to follow the argument, but it jumped and vanished amongst the spatter of words. Everywhere fur and fat juddered in its private dance. The map of bodies pushed on.

When it happened, it was almost imperceptible, and yet no less electric for its subtlety. It was like blood carried on water, infusing every molecule with its trace element. There had been a silent signal, and each sensed it at the same moment. Bristles stiffened; ears pricked. Somewhere, there was screaming.

One by one the militia materialised. They slipped their false furs and silk scarves, stepped out from doorways and from under winter coats: a revelation of fury. They moved through the crowd easily, claws on bellies; teeth in fur. Blood on the tiles gathered pace, pooling then congealing under the lights. Shoppers were reduced to cavities, faces frozen open and forever crying out.

The air was salted and cloying. Hard to breathe, and those at the head of the crowd crammed together in one molten mass of bristle and sinew. Ursula saw feet slapping against the floor, claws useless now against the tiles. A face beside hers was smashed against the unforgiving wall – she looked away – and still the crowd surged on, atoms racing onwards even as the flesh fell away.

She saw a guard with his snout buried ribs-deep in an elegant lady clutching a purse. Others ran, only to be ripped and shredded and fluttered amongst the glassware.

They were lost amongst themselves. Families split, comrades turning. Cubs barked and reached for each other even as their entrails were pulped. The guards shrieked for victory, and victory rebounded through the tunnels in formless, unending waves of joy.

It seemed impossible under the weight, yet Ursula turned her head. A door at the back of the jewellery store was hanging open, just yards away. She lunged through the terrible noise, clawing and kicking ferociously. Behind her someone grasped her fur and a small voice called out – and then she was beyond it and running through the innards of the shop, the smashed exit looming like a broken sun. Bodies pushed past her in the afternoon light, muscles rebounding under their rolls of skin.

Ursula resisted the temptation to drop to all fours. She ran with the wind, circling on street corners and doubling back as far as she dared, until the fear raged against her skull and she turned again and rode on. She wove her steps; unpicked them. She went, once more, the long way.

She crested the hill, swings stilled in their stirrups and the tower blocks timing her sprint. The granite cliff reared up against the sky, the afternoon daisy-bright. She took the stairs three and even four at a time, dropping to her front paws and bounding through the corridors. Still she tangled her route, always moving in great eights. Breath knocking in her ribs, hips shaking the plaster from desiccated walls. Bumble pattern against linoleum. Subterfuge. Futile.

Bears are wily on scent; this is their trade, heightened by sport. One of them was waiting for her in the apartment; a great brown beast in mottled fur, eyes small in his skull and legs crossed delicately behind the dining table. He had a deep scent: oily and salted and strung out on sweat.

The cubs were on the balcony, the glass doors folded around them, pinning them against the railings and the wide expanse of sky. They held their heads low on their chests, frozen figures with only the wind stirring through their fur.

The Bear smiled.

"Hullo," he said, and inspected his nails. "You've been gone an awfully long time. We worried you weren't coming back."

Ursula lay her bag on the table, legs trembling beneath her.

"Something happened today, did you hear? At a mall in Garvin." The Bear tutted. "Such a mess," he said slowly, "such a mess."

His tongue flickered along his jaw. His muzzle was spotted amongst the neat bristles; a dull red stain that curved up in a second, false smile. Ursula dropped her eyes to the carpet, finding the same hue dotted among the woven flowers, burgundy stamen sprouting from the bedroom door.

Afternoon blew into the room and ruffled the table cloth, the scent of coffee and sprouts mingling with dust motes. Playing cards on the floor dropped in a hasty pattern, Jacks leering up in disdain. Somewhere above a radio blared out: news from the coast; cities falling in the North; a pompous marching tune. David lifted his head and darted a furtive glance into the room, salt crystals drying in twin tracks on his face.

The Bear observed Ursula from the corner of his eye.

"Can I see the cubs?"

The Bear looked away, a thin smile playing on his lips.

"Please."

He nodded slowly, as though in time to an unheard melody.

The news was done but the radio played on. Warm day; promise of heat. Far below the balcony the barren river winked and glinted, while the trees shook themselves into umbrellas of shade.

Ursula squatted beside David and Kesha. At first they said nothing and then, one by one, they climbed against her belly and mewled. She looked into their faces and held them, teeth tender against their tiny necks. She raised them to the railings and dropped them into the restless sky. She saw them seem to float – just for an instant – and then they were carried away and were gone.

The sun flared against the door, a crown magnificent in its blazing. There was a roar from deep within the apartment.

The Bear had his claws to the handle. He opened the door and they faced each other, twinned in their shading and the set of their jaws.

Those who talk of a fight to the death talk of luxuries. Reality is a long way down.

The Party

The party was a success. Guests spilled out of the ballroom, women anchored in the hall by the weight of their skirts and the balancing of fans and gloves and delicate china. Buttery light and Indian silks were pressed against the corners of the rooms, reflections waltzing across the parquet.

A string quartet was arranged along the landing, passing Handel down among the crowd while an orchestra played in the other room. Bass notes gave way to quadrilles, which swept into ländlers of the old country; descending scales in infinite series that moved men and women to dancing. Everything had its pulse, and it could be discerned in the movement rippling through the downstairs apartments, lurching between Strauss and solemness; between gaiety and gracious nods.

Marin touched again the pins holding her hair in place; it was a new style, unfamiliar in its weight and the bareness of her neck. She gazed down into the hall at a queer angle and tried to catch the attention of Madam Larsen.

"Oh, Captain!" Marin heard her cry, followed by something that was lost among the thrill of strings. "I'm *so* glad you could come. We did worry about this snow ruining our little party!"

The Captain's coat was deftly removed and placed in a closet, and then the Captain and his wife bent their heads at each other and shared a smile, while laden trays twirled overhead with the grace of summer parasols.

Madam Larsen had already turned to greet other guests.

"We did so worry about this snow ruining our little gathering!"

She shared her private joke once more, and the footman closed the door on the darkness outside.

"But this, this is exquisite."

Marin blinked and looked round. A young lady – somebody's cousin? – was admiring the tiny sapphire suspended against her throat.

"May I?" The hand was already grasping for the stone. "You have a generous admirer!"

Marin blushed twice – once for the insinuation, and again for the secret.

A peal of laughter from below: Madam Larsen was still being glad, and then there was Sebastien at the front door, unsmiling and stamping the ice from his boots.

Marin's hand flew to cup the little sapphire, her head tipped just so to indicate the coming break in conversation, but the cousin carried on impervious. Marin's silk gown was a delicate cut and the shade complementary against her colouring. The house was splendid. The brush strokes that made the portraits on the wall were fine and balanced against the weight of the medium, and on and on into details of nothingness in ever greater magnitude. Marin, wondering what it could mean if brush strokes were balanced against the weight of the medium, came instead to the sudden realisation that the girl was not quite of their set.

"That's really very kind of you." Marin smiled, and stopped her eyes from darting towards the hall.

Finally the cousin was called away and Marin came downstairs, hands spread against the bowl of her skirt amid the crush. Sebastien was leaning against a bookcase.

"I'm glad you came! I thought perhaps the snow ..." She had started speaking warmly, but when he turned to look at her felt foolish and inconsequential.

An allegro picked up behind them, carrying the murmuring of the crowd up into the ceilings and against the cornice. Marin squeezed Sebastien's hand behind her skirt and blushed.

"I'm looking forward to seeing the lake!" she whispered and then, wanting to give the impression of busyness, darted into the crowd nodding greetings at indistinct faces.

"Marin –" Sebastien called after her, and she turned in mid-conversation, eyes shining back at him while she enquired after Mr Felova's twisted ankle.

The quartet fell silent, bows angled in readiness, and the orchestra sent yellow tones spiralling into the lull. Then quarter notes were tumbling from above once more and the crowd was caught in the knot of arpeggios. In the ballroom the unknown cousin was circling in the quadrille, smiling under the weight of some keen observation.

"Marin –" She saw Sebastien's lips making the shape of her name and felt hot under the candles. He beckoned her with two fingers and so, in time to a flute laying a melody against woodwork, she went.

Sebastien was frowning at some speck of dust on his lapel when he said: "I won't be able to accompany you this weekend. I'm sorry for any inconvenience." He glanced away somewhere over her head; it was an easy gesture.

"Oh!" Her hand jumped up as of its own free will and she stifled the movement. "I hope it's nothing serious? Well. It's unfortunate." She laughed shyly. "I was very much looking forward to it. Perhaps the following weekend?"

"That won't be possible, I'm afraid."

"No?"

"No."

The flames blazed on their wicks. The doctor, with his waxy, drooping moustache, lurched alongside them.

"Marin! You're quite the young lady!" The doctor gave them both a significant look. "How is your brother? So far from home! You must miss him terribly."

Marin answered his questions brightly but the doctor was already turning to Sebastien: "What news of this railway business, eh? I heard your father won the contract."

Sebastien nodded. "I'll call on you this week!" he laughed, and they exchanged a brisk handshake in the shadow of the ballroom.

After the doctor had gone Marin said in a low voice: "You're indisposed?"

"Not unwilling, Marin. But I'm not available." He saw the stricken look that passed over her face and felt an involuntary thrill. "I'm sorry."

She shook her head and said, "Thank you. Not at all."

Sebastien turned to watch the dancers, partners spinning across the floor, skirts spread wide in invitation. Marin, swallowed by the throng, nodded at couples without seeing faces, was swept away and past the drawing room while the strings droned on. Finally she came to rest and grasped a wall.

"Are you unwell?"

Agnés, who had once been the Lady Szabo, carried tiny chocolates on a plate and looked concerned. She placed a hand on Marin's waist and said, "Perhaps you need to sit down? Dancing can be too much, for some."

"I –" Marin stared wildly about the room, at the people surging past and the waltzing couples beyond.

Agnés steered her to an unused parlour at the rear of the house. She pressed her handkerchief into Marin's hand.

"Perhaps I should get your mother?" She spoke softly in the unlit room and it seemed ominous, the party behind them both and locked away.

"Please – no."

"But you're unwell? Some water, at least."

Marin looked at her hopelessly. "I was to visit the frozen lake this weekend. With a young man."

Agnés smoothed the moulded pleats in her gown and thought a moment. "Ah, yes."

"But he is unable to keep the engagement." The words came stiffly, as though through frozen lips.

Agnés took Marin's hand, and the lines in her face softened into some aspect of sympathy.

"You poor girl," she said. "You had an understanding?" She rolled her eyes when Marin shook her head. There was always an understanding: some chose not to lay it open in fairness, and others chose not to inspect it.

"No. There was nothing untoward; I am not ill-used. I am just –" Marin tried to shrug, to gesture at the ceiling or at God, but the neck of her gown pulled tight and held her in place. "If I am not suitable, what can I do?"

"Nothing," Agnés agreed. "You can't create kindness where there is none."

Marin was silent. Her eyes skated across the room: chairs cloaked in the grey; framed portraits resting wordlessly against the walls. She straightened her shoulders.

"What else is there, then, except to maintain some grace?"

"Of course," said Agnés, "Of course." She squeezed the girl's waist and left with her chocolates; she turned the corner and was gone amid the light and the music, carrying the news to her friends.

Marin waited in the dark. She toyed with unkind words, brought them out halfway, heard the noise of them and imagined how they would look clawing at Sebastien. Then she saw them spent and ineffectual against his shirt. All for nothing.

Madam Larsen came to mind; the indomitable Madam Larsen who, in her youth, was refused by a politician and consequently smashed her mirror in his face, giving him the scar which even now graced his profile on postage stamps. And after the event? The politician returned, courting her until she threw him aside to become Madam Larsen. It was hard to imagine the great lady caught with neither understanding nor invitation; she would have demanded clarity.

But the matter is already ended! The thought chased after her and she blinked it away, momentarily stunned by the din at the front of the house. Sebastien was nodding his leave, caught briefly in the frame of the front door as it closed behind him. The strings swelled over the party, glasses clinked percussively, and the evening reached its crescendo.

Marin's skirt was crushed, creases jumping through the silk and the slow horror of a wine stain dropped from great height. She covered it with her hand and threw open the door, and the swirling, frosted night rushed in.

She felt the bitterness on her cheeks before she saw the snow pushed up against the steps, and stood for a moment undecided. Then she hurtled into the evening and pulled the door behind her, and was in the street, alone.

She stretched her neck against the black and stars; she looked this way and that, finally calling out to the figure striding ahead.

"Marin – are you mad? You'll get ill. Go inside at once."

"Why?" The word juddered in the cold like a glass bead.

"Because it's snowing and you don't even have a shawl –"

"Why are you breaking your invitation? What have I done?"

Sebastien peered down at her from under raised eyebrows.

"Marin, I already apologised. It wasn't my intention to wound you. I didn't want you to misunderstand the situation is all; I didn't want to mislead you. This seems unnecessary."

"I haven't come after you to change your mind."

She held her head as stiffly as she could while her teeth chattered and her body shook in violence.

"You enjoyed my company, and I yours, and now here you are without any … without any warning, telling me I shouldn't even approach you in future."

"I said nothing of the kind."

"In those words, no. But you have no intention of seeing me again. Do you? Do you?"

"Would it have been any easier for you with a month's notice? Or three? Is it my telling you that upsets you, or the timing? I can't help either."

Snow fell among her lashes and melted.

"Your feeling," she said hoarsely, "is your own. But as someone for whom you must surely have some regard, you could speak plainly now. That is the least token of regard."

"Very well. I'm getting married."

Marin was still for so long that the snow inched a watermark clear up the hem of her dress, indelible. She dropped her hands in defeat and the wine stain was spread and multiplied by others made fresh under the open sky.

But how? How could something of such magnitude be held in private for so long and revealed so begrudgingly?

"To whom?" she asked.

"What difference would it make?" He shivered beneath his coat and tapped his fingers against a pocket for warmth.

Marin blinked at him, his face shifting and doubled in eddies of snow and fine grit. A thousand injustices came to mind but everything she might have howled for seemed redundant and improper.

Ice was frosting over his buttons and Sebastien looked down at her, not with distaste, but like a man standing in another room. The image of Madam Larsen grew dim and suddenly Marin found herself in the street in a ruined dress and crooked chignon.

"I see," she said. "I see – and I wish you –" but the charming bestowal of happiness was mangled by her frozen mouth and came out an unintelligible slur.

Even as she turned to leave clever words came close behind her. She felt the injustices again – and then night pushed her on. She wrapped the words and took them with her.

Sebastien watched her leave, her slippers skating over the blue ice and the hem of her skirt blackened and awful. She half-slid towards the house, arms flailing for balance as she went and loops of hair plastered against her shoulders, and then she was disappeared in the darkness.

Sebastien stood looking after her for a few minutes, and then he too turned to go. It could have been an embarrassing scene but Marin had shown great dignity. He nodded to himself. Yes, she was impressive. He repeated it twice and, to his credit, thought about her as far as the corner, and then his thoughts turned to railways and contract issues, and a deep concern for the weather.

Company Business

November, and a letter had arrived. Heavy cream paper, it read in entirety:

```
Delighted to offer you the job. Report to the
Danver office, December 16th. In meantime,
all congratulations.

P. Crujo,
Operations Manager
```

Martha put her head beside Famke's, stealing the words over his shoulder.

"Delighted to offer you the job? What job? You didn't tell me!" She had her arms around him now – almost.

Famke shrugged. "I haven't applied for anything."

She pressed her body against his, but the whisper had come and fled in the thin space between them; laying doubt, telling tales.

The clock on the mantel chased 8.14. Famke turned the letter over, as though misplaced memory might be etched on its back. He scratched his chin through beard: "It mustn't be for me."

But the envelope implied it *was* for him. 'Mr Famke', and there was their address in spare, linear type.

Martha held it up to the light.

"This is addressed to Mr Famke."

"So?"

"So it could be a typo. Perhaps it was intended for Mrs Famke."

Famke turned to her in surprise. "You! You applied for a job?"

"I'm just saying. It might not be for either of us."

"True. Perhaps, it's someone's idea of a joke." He went to grind the hilarity in his fist, and then found he didn't want to. The paper was so fine, so expensive. There was a weight, even, in its economy of wording.

The letter itself contained only the words they had read. The frank on the envelope showed an eagle in flight above the legend 'Danver Technological Industries, Danver'.

Martha shivered on the doormat, tiny beneath two jumpers, and asked why a body would go to so much trouble for a lark.

"For the usual reasons," Famke said, and trembled over the band of his trousers. He thought of the family who had gone on holiday in good faith, and returned to find their house bulldozed and rebuilt – shoddily – in a field four miles away. Or the woman, once, who allowed herself to be courted, fell in love, left her job, moved to Cradensk, got engaged, planned the wedding and then there, in front of her friends and family, and in full formal dress, received the punchline. The groom that turned up for the wedding was a stranger with papers proving he was, without doubt, the real Jonah Ostin. Of the other Ostin – the one she'd courted – there was no sign, on that day or any that followed. The whole thing had been a set-up, and her friends and family had been in on it. You could call that elaborate, when it took months in the planning, and years in the making.

So the letter was a prank, and yet they dawdled on the doormat.

"What would Danver Technological Industries want with me!" Famke puffed.

"What even do they do?" Martha had never heard of them; they neither of them had.

"I suppose it doesn't matter."

Martha was unconvinced. "Shouldn't we let them know? Perhaps this other Famke is waiting to hear about the job he applied for?"

"How? There's no return address. Besides, if they never meant to send it in the first place we'll look like idiots." No, he shook his head – that wouldn't do.

Famke drove to the office through sleet, the wipers tutting at the screen, and ice packed under the wheels of the tin-pot Hylanda. The morning dragged, and Famke twice found himself in the stairwell, pulling the letter out and reading, in entirety:

```
Delighted to offer you the job. Report to the
Danver office, December 16th. In meantime,
all congratulations.

P. Crujo,
Operations Manager
```

It was a strange thing, to carry the words in his pocket and know they weren't meant for him, and yet their promise was contagious.

He lined up the pencils on his desk according to size, and then Belma reached over for the shortest – sharpened over the year into a fat stump – and asked had he not been peckish again?

Belma had a face like a vole, so what should he care? Still, everyone laughed. If the letter were really for him he might have reached over and poured tea into her typewriter, or gurned maniacal, idiot faces at her.

At lunchtime he hefted himself to the information office upstairs and pulled down the stacks of reference books. There were three volumes for Danver. Famke spread them across the table and worked their pages methodically. The capital city reared up in paper and digits and facts piled all around him, towers of constructed imagining given bones and then business by his reading – but there was nothing about any Danver Technological Industries.

He sat back and scratched his chin. He could see the others below, sharp back from lunch and bent over their paperwork. One last surge of urgency and then there it was: Danver Technological Industries, 1445 The Avenue, Danver 01145-B. No phone number. No board members. No accounts. No clue as to what they did with all their time.

Late back from lunch and the juddering of the metal stairs sure to draw every critical eye; he knew and dreaded it – yet he'd learned that there really was such a company as Danver Technological Industries, and that it had a real physical address. Of the rest of it all – how he'd come into possession of a letter, and whether it was an error or an evil – he didn't know, yet it gave the afternoon a sense of accomplishment.

It was an accomplishment that stretched the day thin and soon pasted it once more across the Hylanda's windscreen. The letter was placed in a drawer beneath Famke's best underpants and socks. Later it was a game the two of them played over dinner – the detective plot of who and why – and then they turned their attention to fried beans, the radio coughing and whispering behind them.

A couple of weeks later, another shadow on the doormat.

Martha called excitedly from the front door, him still crunching bacon in its pastry blanket, coffee on his shirt.

"Look here!" she cried, "another letter – and there's a cheque!"

Famke reached for the envelope. It was stiff-backed, typed and franked the same as the first.

"Why did you open it?"

"Why shouldn't I? You didn't apply for the job – or any job, you said."

"So?"

"So it's not for you then, is it?"

"It's addressed to me." His voice steamed against the glass panel in the door.

"Then I won't open it next time. OK?" She peered up at him. "So tell me truthfully, then."

Famke raised his eyebrows and waited.

"Did you apply for a job without telling me?"

He'd been unreasonable. He'd spoken harshly.

"No, of course not. You're right enough – it's just a typing error."

She smiled in the corner of her mouth. "Either way, the cheque's addressed to you."

So it was. The cheque was made out to Mr Famke, and it would more than cover two months' rent.

```
Please find enclosed a reimbursement of
travel expenses. We look forward to welcoming
you to the Danver office, December 16th.

P. Crujo,
Operations Manager
```

"They pay this just for travel expenses? It's a shame you didn't apply for the job."

Famke was silent. Then he replied to no one:

"But I can't cash it."

"No. I mean, of course not. It's not meant for you. It's just addressed to you. Here. At this address. That's odd, isn't it? The chances of getting your name wrong, and getting your address wrong at the same time ... so that both turn out to be correct ... well, that's odd, isn't it?"

"Must be a million to one. Something like that."

They stood looking at each other while the fat on the breakfast plates hardened over.

Famke fetched a writing pad and sat at the table. He wiped the nib of the pen against the back of his hand and thought what to write. It took a few attempts because his style seemed never quite to match Crujo's oddly terse politeness, and then because Martha pointed out that 'Mr' Crujo might be no such thing.

"He could be a she, why not?"

"Quite right, Mrs Famke, quite right." Famke struck it out, and then it was done.

```
Thank you for your letters. Unfortunately
they appear to have been misdirected – I am
not the Famke that applied for the job. I am
returning both letters, and your cheque.

Sincerely,
P. Famke
```

They read it over three times apiece and nodded at each other. Famke folded it, placed it in the original envelope with a fresh stamp, and wrote along its bottom edge: For attention of Crujo, c/o Danver Technological Industries, Danver.

They walked together to the corner of the street and dropped it into the mailbox. They stood a while looking down into the recess, the letter hidden amid a hundred others. It was gone 8.30 by then, so they turned on the corner and went their separate ways, footsteps diverging and, finally, lost on the busy thoroughfare.

Letter. Letters. A deluge. Everything returned with elastic speed. Their letter to the Danver company came back first, Famke's careful printing ruined under an official stamp: 'Address incomplete'. Someone had corrected his effort below that in blue ink: *Use the postal code!*

Famke rolled his eyes, but made a note to return to the information office and retrieve the full address. They propped the cheque beside the clock; a beautiful, redundant bauble.

Then, a fresh letter:

```
Due to restructuring report to Cradensk
office, January 4th. Please find enclosed fee
for inconvenience, and accept apologies for
the same. We look forward to welcoming you to
Danver Technological Industries (Cradensk).

P. Crujo,
Operations Manager (Danver)
```

Martha was dismayed.

"Cradensk? That's hundreds of miles away!"

Famke laughed to see her face. "What difference does it make?"

They put the second cheque on the mantel and stood over it sorrowfully. It was an extravagant amount, both ridiculous and somehow real.

Famke used the phone in Luborger's office to call the Bureau of Information. His finger shook in the dial because he didn't know when Luborger would be back.

"Number?"

Famke tucked a whisper into the receiver, one hand over his mouth: "Danver Techno-"

"Sir? Which number?"

He coughed and fired his request at the invisible ear, then waited while the line went mute. He jiggled his weight over his feet and tried not to see Luborger's private life cradled on the shelves.

"That number is withheld."

Famke stopped jiggling.

"How can it be private? It's a business!"

"Do you require another number, sir?"

He placed the receiver in its holster and gnawed at his thumb. If the number was withheld, then a number existed. Perhaps it was some kind of state contractor, an organisation that didn't need to be found? On the other hand, if someone was trying to give the sheen of appearance to a nasty prank, what better outfit to hide behind than one that was unknowable and unverifiable?

"What are you doing in here?"

Famke gave a girlish scream.

"I ..."

Luborger, with his nicotine fingers, looked at him with distaste. Famke opened his mouth several times, a man drowning in ineptitude, or struggling with the stink suddenly emanating from his own armpits.

"I ..."

"Yes," Luborger snapped, gaze swiftly searching the office. "You. What are you doing in here?"

"Sir! I ... came to make a complaint."

Luborger's eyes narrowed. "Oh?"

In truth, incidents stretched back over the years like a low, static hum; the fruits of a lazy intimidation at the hands of his colleagues. Famke had wavered between wanting not to care, and wanting to strip the skins from his tormentors; seeing it as playful affection – and then naming it as his torture. But all was too late; all had slept too long without voice, which meant now it was not truly his for calling.

Famke gave a summary of sorts while Luborger picked the dirt from under his nails. Luborger wrote something on a notepad and nodded sagely several times. Finally he looked up:

"Get out."

Afterwards Luborger proceeded to act quickly and decisively – by which he did nothing, and told everything. Famke's sector had heard and digested the complaint racket by the day's end. Belma wasn't talking to Famke, but that simply meant she had no more words for him than usual, and louder, more effusive comments for everyone else.

Famke stepped into the storm igniting above the car park, rain coming fresh and with fury. Even in the dead evening light he could make out the scratch along the length of the car. A 'Management Welcomes Your Feedback' card lay in a wrapper on the windscreen. The wiper had been curled into a salute.

Inside, on the passenger seat, lay the kind of out-sized bicycle horn most typically found in circus tents – a metal curlicue topped by a bulbous rubber lung. Famke was surprised despite everything: that they'd had time to find such a thing at such short notice. He went to start the engine and then stopped abruptly, his hand jumping to the passenger door. It had been forced open, no tenderness expressed on the shattered lock.

Famke drove home with his face pressed against the windscreen and his belt hooked between the broken lock and a head rest. As he cut across the 45-Turnpike, the door flapped in the gale like a stoic applauding.

Famke announced he would go to the Danver company in person.

"In Cradensk?" Martha asked.

Cradensk was too far to correct someone else's error, Famke said. He'd go to the Danver office and find Crujo. He'd return the cheques, minus the cost of getting there and back. That seemed a fair compromise.

Martha was downhearted. "When will you go?"

"As soon as I can get leave. I could be back before the weekend's done, even." He grinned an apology. "Don't worry, Mrs Famke. Next time we'll go to Cradensk together. Next holiday."

They laughed, because there hadn't been any holiday since there had been a Mrs Famke; not since their honeymoon in the next town over. So instead Martha crawled next to him on the sofa and hid her face in his beard for a while.

Luborger was less welcoming of the idea. He raked his hands through his hair as though battling inner demons, or lice.

"It's short notice." Luborger fixed his eyes on the folds of Famke's neck. "Do you even care how this department's workload is achieved?"

Whether he cared or not, Famke was owed leave – and so he took it. By the time Martha came home that evening his suitcase was by the door and the cheque and its cashed sibling was in the pocket of his Arctic Adventurer coat.

"Think of it this way: the car's all yours while I'm gone – no more snow shuffling!" His hand went to his pocket and came out with a couple of clean bills – in case she had time to drive it to the garage, he said.

They hugged on the doorstep, and then Famke was gone to Danver.

The city was a lie. The first was to suggest 'The Avenue' could be a singular thing. There were at least eight of them arranged in radial spokes around Grand Central station alone. Famke picked one at random and scoured the hoardings for a cheap hotel. He walked slowly – regretting the Arctic coat that ballooned around him – like a baby seal stuffed into a sleeping bag.

The Hotel Madeline had nothing of propriety about it, and even less familiarity with hygiene. The room on the third floor had a bed, a washstand, and someone else's underpants balled under the mattress. There was a shared bathroom with communal fetid stink at the end of the hall.

Famke walked down to the café on the corner and asked to use the phone. The owner picked urgently at his nose and asked did Famke intend to eat? Famke didn't, but ordered black coffee, which came in a greasy cup and was gone in two swallows. He flipped his pennies into the saucer and asked again about the phone.

"Payphone." The owner dragged his hands over his dirty apron and nodded at the booth. "Three quarters to place a call."

"Three? The coffee cost less than one?"

"Then don't use it. This isn't the post office."

Famke dropped the coins into the metal box. He heard the dial tone bouncing cross-country, and then Martha's voice in the receiver.

"Hello?"

"Martha –" and then the pips were going. By the time he'd reached for another coin the line was dead.

"Hey," he called across the empty tables, "I got cut off."

The owner gave a violent shrug. "Three-quarter minimum."

"I put in three quarters."

"Three-quarter minimum each call! Have you used a phone before? Do they have them where you come from?"

Famke couldn't get a word in after that. The owner riffed long and lyrically about Famke's ability to use the phone, and the part of the world in which Famke typically was to be found. As Famke hustled for the door he screamed after him, "This isn't a supermarket!"

Famke went back to the room and emptied his coins on the bedspread. Where they his, or the company's? Either way, there were fewer of them.

He pinned the remaining cheque to the lining of the Arctic coat and bundled it into the wardrobe. He stood at the window and watched the traffic sliding up and down the avenue, listening to the muted strains of traffic and hunger. He wondered what Martha was doing and, for a moment, she seemed to appear against the reflections in the window, suspended between theatre lights and exhaust plumes. She smiled, and Famke found himself waving back.

The morning's job was simply to locate Danver Technological Industries.

"I'm looking for The Avenue."

The night porter – still on shift and yawning in his booth – didn't look up. "You're on it."

"No, but ... no. Excuse me, sir? I'm looking for Danver Technological Industries."

The porter closed his eyes. "Maps are a quarter," and then, through his yawn, something about where Famke could find one: "... café on the corner."

Without a map it took until noon to find the building. The endeavour was like trying to lasso thin air, and it involved trudging a great spiral, asking directions every few blocks, and creeping up on The Avenue as though it wouldn't stand for direct gaze.

The eastern quarter was a carbuncle of urban planning. Streets which led into themselves. Empty plots. Industrial pits. Schools.

Cheap high-rise blocks stacked against the sky, and a landlocked quay. It was a city of its own kind.

Then the streets took breath and widened out. A few cars here and there; a body scurrying alongside a tattered briefcase. Buildings which at one junction shamelessly exposed their plumbing and innards gave way to dark stone and glass fronts, and the landscape rushed towards modernity.

The Danver office was a monolith rising out of the broken tarmac, geometric and crystalline. It split the sun across several planes and handed it down piece by piece. Inside, though, the lobby was gloomy, strip lights tucked away in recesses as though clarity were a very yesterday thing.

There was a collection of plastic chairs on stumpy legs, and a marbled interior that had the look of fissures and cracks, and gave an impressive sense of the weight of the building hanging overhead. And white – everything in shades of white so that chairs and walls merged like secret panels, and the woman behind the curved reception desk appearing to float legless somewhere at waist height.

She smiled as Famke approached, her head on one side as though she'd miscalculated the weight of her immaculate bun.

"I'm here to see Crujo," Famke announced. "Operations Manager."

"Mr Crujo is in Cradensk."

Famke was dismayed. "He's been transferred?"

"He's there this week. He'll be back on Monday." She looked at him cautiously. "You heard about Cradensk?"

Famke found himself shrugging expansively. "Me! I just got a letter telling me to report to Cradensk next month. Cradensk!"

The woman glanced around the deserted lobby: "It's not right. A letter, indeed! No class. Perhaps management should go to Cradensk!"

Famke ran his hands though his hair. "I mean, do you even care how this department is run!"

"Right!" she laughed, and Famke was close enough to see she did indeed have legs back there under her maroon skirt suit. She had a tiny pin on her lapel that identified her as J. Smarky, and suddenly Famke wondered what kind of hole he'd made for himself. J. Smarky coughed, and he quickly removed his gaze from her chest.

"You see the thing is, Miss, er –"

"Miss-ez," she sang quickly, "Miss-ez."

"The thing is, Mrs Smarky, there's been a bit of a mix-up."

"Oh?" She sounded doubtful.

"Yes. You see, I won't be going to Cradensk – I shouldn't even be here. I keep getting letters about a job I didn't apply for."

"Which job?" She materialised a stack of papers from behind the desk and stood poised.

"I don't know."

"No – for which job did you apply?"

"I didn't apply for any job. That's what I'm saying. I didn't apply for any job."

Smarky spoke slowly now, enunciating the words. "You didn't apply for a job, but you got a letter telling you to go to Cradensk, so you came here. To Danver." Frozen smile, vowels insinuating Famke was a moron.

"I got a letter," Famke spoke just as slowly, "about a job I didn't apply for. And when I sent it back to Mr Crujo, I got another letter telling me to go to Cradensk."

He sighed a retreat. "Perhaps it would be best if I talked to Mr Crujo directly. On Monday."

J. Smarky gave a full smile. "Perhaps that would be best! I'll be sure to tell him you called, Mr …?"

"Famke."

"Mr Famke." She turned to her paperwork.

Famke hesitated and then said again, "Famke."

"Yes." Smarky was clipped now, through her grin. "Mr Famke."

The empty space above seemed to rush at him, promising annihilation – and yet he'd come all this way.

"I'm sorry, but I can't tell if you're saying Fanke or Famke. With an 'M'?"

Smarky stopped smiling.

"With an 'F'!"

Famke nodded. He was tired. He hadn't eaten since the train. He'd come all this way, and Crujo – if he existed at all – was in Cradensk.

He reached the door when he heard Smarky barking after him. The sound of his name once more was a torture.

"Mr Crujo left a letter for you. You may as well take it now."

She held the envelope out to him, and there was his name and his address; a talisman of the real world.

Famke took it and stood without moving. He was too frightened to speak and then, finally, he begged her pardon, but could she spare him some paper and an envelope? Smarky could, and when she slapped them down on the desk, the sound ricocheted through the lobby like a pistol shot.

The week in Danver dragged. They were lean days summed out of silver quarters. Breakfast was a sausage or ham, coffee on high days. Lunch was the aroma of street carts selling charred, sugar-crusted nuts. Supper was bread and pickles taken in the flare of theatre lights across the way. In between there was a never-ending circuit through the streets. He came to know the names of the subway routes; roamed in the shopping district and the spice market; saw the first catch hauled in on rusted hulls; and learned to locate the constellations.

Crujo's letter during this time was a mythic portent. Famke found himself carrying it with him through the city's nestled districts, unopened and in his pocket.

Instead he sat and tried to write something useful to Martha, and that too became a practice of procrastination. He composed whole scenes and sentiments while out walking, but found that the dirty room sucked the ink from his intent each evening.

Finally he borrowed a pencil from the night porter, put himself on the corner of the bed, and arranged his thoughts.

```
Martha, I've come all this way, only to find
Crujo has left town! I'm to wait for his return,
and am hopeful of clearing up this whole affair
next week. I'll return soonest –
```

and so it ran, with amends and addenda about talking to Luborger, and what to keep an eye on with the car. He signed it with a lead kiss, and went to bed feeling quite dejected.

December brought false winter to Danver. The days were bright, and snow appeared only to ever fall at night. Famke found it in the mornings, grey and gutter-side, but never witnessed it made fresh. Still, it was cold enough to savour the Arctic coat, which grew like a loose skin around him as he receded from his girth. He patrolled the streets gathering clumps of city grit in his beard and, for the first time, it disgusted him.

He bought a razor and hacked at the matted hair, cutting it back until he could reach his face. Afterwards he stared at himself in the mirror, strangely bald and fleshy, and with the illusion of two heads, one hanging despondently beneath the other.

On Sunday evening Famke opened Crujo's letter and then sat holding both heads in despair.

```
Project delayed. Report to Cradensk office,
February – date to be advised. Please find the
enclosed, free of obligation, in advance of your
start date. We look forward to welcoming you to
Danver Technological Industries (Cradensk).

P. Crujo,
Operations Manager (Danver)
```

The cheque, in lieu of a delayed first salary, was four times his monthly earnings. Famke placed it beside its twin and stowed supper in its plastic wrapper.

"How may I help you?" Mrs Smarky smiled her false-fronted welcome.

"I'm here to see Crujo."

"I'm sorry, sir; Mr Crujo is in Cradensk."

"But you said he would be here today."

Smarky peered across the counter and then seemed to recoil.

"Oh!" She gazed at his cascading chins in dismayed wonder. "But he's not here."

Famke clenched his fists inside his coat.

"When will he be back?"

"Monday," Smarky said. "Come back on Monday."

He buried the afternoon at the harbour, watching gulls dive for chum. The city was inverted in oil slicks, recast in rainbows while the sea – addling under ice – turned slowly black. Behind fishing vessels crowding for berth lay a panoply of tankers in their matt shells, and container ships stacked with corrugated packages. Static ships moored to the landscape, but still they'd seen Africa and the far side of the world.

The facts as they appeared were that Famke was in Danver. Crujo was in Cradensk. Luborger would be pissed, but he was hardly pleasant at the best of times.

He could go home, he realised; he *should* go home. He could go home and they could cash the cheques – was that fraud? The company had promised him a job, and everything he had done so far had been in response to that. If they asked for the money he could work it back at the Cradensk office exactly as had been suggested; he'd been nothing but amenable so far.

Gulls circled and cried out, battling for scraps and jetsam cast upon the water. Famke shivered in his coat. He'd lived on nothing and sandwiched his girth every evening into a single bed, and yet technically he was on company business. Danver Technological Industries had engaged his services – albeit mistakenly – and here he was, set in motion because of it. The more he thought it, the more compelling it seemed. He rubbed his chin, the hint of tomorrow's stubble asserting itself.

What was the job, anyway? It must be dark dealings, for such salary and secrecy. Industrial espionage. Insider trading. Shady investments. Something worse? Hired assassin. Union breaker. It was all very well writing off the stolen cheques as something he could pay back: what if the payback was beyond his threshold or ability? Caught in the vice, his coat pockets flapping like good gossip.

He spent the last of the coins on chestnuts and ate them as he walked, warming his fingers on their hot cases and spitting fibres into the street. He drew level with a woman in a fur-lined hood and they played the dance of let-me-pass.

"How can I get by with a fat lump like you in the way?" Spider lines flared around her mouth and spread a pattern of gouges across her cheeks.

He found himself grasping her elbow.

"Go around me then!" he bellowed, and launched her like a toboggan along the pavement. She sailed past him in her boots, mouth working a redundant gasp. She slid to a rest and clung to the glass of a department store window, then scurried on without a backwards glance.

Famke stood for a moment, trembling and ashamed. He rolled the chestnuts in their bag and waited for the indignation to subside.

The night porter, already tucked into his booth, looked up as Famke came in.

"There was a phone call about you."

Famke spoke carefully: "A woman?"

"Yes. She was checking you could be contacted here." The porter gave a sly grin.

"What did she say?"

"She didn't say anything. She just asked if this is where you could be reached."

"Then why bother telling me!" Famke thumped his hands on the counter, eyes popping in their folds of skin.

The porter looked unimpressed. He leaned towards Famke.

"Do you mind if I say something?"

"Say it."

"It suits you, this new look. That old beard did nothing for you. You've shaved ten years off your face!"

The porter's name was Marcel, and it turned out he was from Torssen, not fifty miles from Famke's place. Standing up he was surprisingly lanky. He insisted Famke join him in the booth, the two of them wedged behind the counter and passing a petrol-like vintage between themselves as the clock found 5.

"So that's it? Leaving on the night train like a fugitive?"

"What else can I do?"

"Cash your cheque and spend your last night in a decent hotel. I should tell you who had your room before you!" Marcel got busy with the bottle. "No," he said eventually, "it's not Freud. It's company business. You've been in Danver for days and haven't even seen the Finkelstein Gallery. Or the view from Margoli Point. Or Club Blue Note. You've been feeding birds and waiting for this Famke character."

"Crujo," Famke crooned.

"Exactly, my friend; exactly."

They toasted each other solemnly and tipped their mugs.

"What would you have done?"

"Me?" Marcel closed one eye and thought. "This."

```
Thank you for the kind offer of a job with
your company, and your letters confirming
the same. Based on the one that came before
the last one I had in fact already arranged
travel and other considerations. I arrive
in Cradensk imminently, and trust you will
arrage interim duties, if not actual duties,
relating to the duties under consideration.

I look forward to starting my new role and
am confident of making a splash with Danver
Technological Industries (Cradensk).

In sincerity,
Famke
```

Famke scratched his cheek. He didn't know that he'd ever 'make a splash', but Marcel was adamant.

"This is how these corporate types talk!"

"But," said Famke desperately, "I'm not going to Cradensk. I have a wife. I can't afford to go to Cradensk. And besides – I don't even know what Danver Technological Industries do. What if they think they're hiring a lawyer? Or an accountant? They could be expecting a chief medical officer!"

Marcel shrugged. "So do what everyone else does: fake it and go to night school. You think I actually managed security for the Torssen Highways Authority before this?" He waited for Famke's frown. "Exactly. There is no Torssen Highways Authority.

"Listen. Don't worry about your room rent tonight." He went to tap the side of his nose and missed. "I'll square things with the manager, with Mr ...." He clicked his fingers but the name escaped him. "Anyway, tonight, I'm showing you the city. The best way to see any city is at night, you know."

"Under the lights?"

"In the dark, my friend."

Famke shook his head and the lobby seemed to rise and fall like a wave.

"You can't leave without seeing the Blue Note."

Famke brought out a handful of chestnuts and threw them on the counter.

"Sure," he gestured, "Let's go crazy."

Marcel sighed and drew out a wad of paper bills and pennies. He peeled off a note and held it up, swaying under the lights.

"This. This is your train ticket to Cradensk. And this –" another note "– is your share of the drinks tonight." He pushed them into Famke's hand. "Take it. Go to Cradensk. If you can make it work you cash those cheques and you pay me back. If you can't, you're on your own. OK?" He pulled his coat from the back of the chair and wrestled himself into it.

For a moment, Marcel's face was blurred.

"Why would you do that?"

Marcel's eyebrows jumped up on his forehead.

"Why wouldn't I?"

Famke turned away to clear his throat.

"Isn't it early? Will this club even be open yet?"

"Of course not. We're not going straight there."

They stumbled through the empty streets; Saturday evening, and store folk long gone. Marcel threw his hands in the air and ran and slid, like a boy discovering the properties of ice for the very first time.

Then Marcel was pulling Famke up-hill and gradually the peachy lights of Danver stretched out below. They were in the shadow of a high concrete wall; it stretched grey and forever in a curve and Famke breathed heavily and asked where they were.

"Come on!" Marcel raced ahead into the evening.

Famke found himself alone and panting after shadows. He thought he saw Marcel waving ahead, and fell into the gaping mouth of the wall and was suddenly in black space.

"Marcel?" His voice echoed and floated around him.

"Come on!" Marcel called from somewhere ahead, and then Famke saw his silhouette, thin and elastic against the mouth of the tunnel. He stumbled on, and the blackness and the roaring in his ears gave way and everything was still and silent. He was in another space – a great open one – aware once more of snow falling, and the cold kiss of iced air.

"Where are you?"

It was as though a false sun had ignited in the heavens and the world had turned white. Famke blinked. He'd never even seen the inside of a stadium, yet here he was on the grass pitch with seats rising around him in a great parabola, bone-bleached under the floodlights.

Marcel was running towards him, coat flapping in his wake. He launched the ball at Famke; it smacked him in the face and he stood, stunned.

"Kick it!" Marcel raced past, breath heavy in his throat and coming out in smoky plumes.

"Aren't there guards?"

"There will be!"

Famke broke into a fast walk and came up on the ball. He lifted his leg uncertainly.

"We're trespassing," Marcel shouted. "You want to go to jail?"

Famke kicked the ball and it curved wide and flew a few feet. Marcel whooped and pulled the tail of his coat over his head. Famke watched him race along the pitch, a great black bird swooping under the stars. The booze burn was heavy in his belly. Everything was possible.

Morning leered in at the window. Famke tried to sit up, and immediately lay down again. Something in his head had broken and was rattling loose, punching up against his brain. He couldn't remember climbing into the sagging single bed; he didn't even remember getting back to the hotel. He closed his eyes quickly, but the nausea was unshakeable.

Famke fell out of bed still tangled in the Arctic coat. He unravelled himself and stumbled to the wash stand and vomited long and loudly. He slumped his head against the mirror and washed the pattern of last night into the drain. He leaned. And laughed. Here was life! Here was life, racing down the plug hole and into the sewer on Sunday morning!

He mopped the room with a towel labelled 'Property of Ingmar Comfort Station' – the hotel on the corner. He worked with gusto and unexpected cheeriness, flicking decades of dust from the skirting board and whistling. It was a stranger's face that seemed to watch him from the mirror as he went about his business. Without his beard he looked quite disapproving, he realised. Perhaps that was a good thing?

The woman from the icy sidewalk came to mind of a sudden, and he blushed a second dawn. He thought about Marcel, and how there are good people, and bad people, and how some folk are a bit of both, and that's the most you can hope for. He rolled his clothes into their customary knot and stowed them in the bottom of his bag.

Marcel wasn't in his booth. The crow-faced boy he'd materialised into over night nodded at a fig tree growing in a gilt bucket. Behind that, stuffed into an armchair and beneath a blanket of Business Times Today, was Marcel. It took just five jabs to wake him, and then he peered out from under the pages with a sorrowful expression, and breaking news inked across his forehead.

"So you're off, are you?" Marcel winced and pressed his skull as if waiting for the glue to dry. "Off to Cradensk, eh? Tomorrow is here for you today, my friend!"

Famke watched the floor. "I should go home. I have a wife."

"You have a wife," Marcel agreed. "I thought you were going to Cradensk, not joining the circus. So what, you have a wife? I thought you wanted this job?"

But that wasn't right, Famke thought. He tried to resurrect fragments of the previous evening. Surely he'd never claimed to want this job – or any of the events of the past month? He'd been trying to rectify a series of errors, but the errors had overtaken him and now here he was a tenant of his own winter coat.

"I have a job," he said, but sounded doubtful.

"With the idiot Luborger." Marcel closed his eyes. "Yes, best get yourself back there. Best ... run along."

Famke was surprised to hear Luborger's name. So he'd shared more than he'd realised. Perhaps he'd confessed to wanting the Cradensk job? He shook his head. It wasn't true, he knew, because there was no job – there was only its shadow.

"I can't take your money." He slid a bank note onto Marcel's bony knee: "We blew the other one on booze."

Each spent a moment with his own recollection of vodka curdling in milk, and blanched a little.

"I believe we donated most of it to a young lady's under-funded wardrobe situation," Marcel added.

Famke had a sudden, startling memory – there had been lights, and music, and a woman dancing on a stage in greying, functional underwear. And there had been football. He stood up abruptly.

"Listen," he said, "Listen. You should let me know when you're next in Torssen. I'll show you my place. You'll like Martha."

"Who's Martha?"

Famke ignored the sinking feeling. "My wife."

"Oh, right. Sure, sure. And how am I to let you know?"

"I'll give you my number."

Famke patted his pockets for a full minute before Marcel smirked and pulled out a pen. He scribbled on the crumpled bank note and handed it back to Famke formally.

"My direct line. Let me know if you make it back in one piece." He pulled the newspaper over his face and, from beneath Business Times Today, smiled to himself and gently snored.

Famke stopped at the café on the corner and made business-like show of using the phone. He heard the coins bouncing in the slot, and then – as though such a thing could be true – heard them take flight and soar along the wires, racing east across the plains like bright-winged birds.

He'd mulled the thought in some detail before realising the phone was still ringing. Where could she be? He glanced at the clock on the wall. Of course, she'd be shopping at this time. How long since he'd called Martha? Not since the day he'd arrived in Danver. No – that was the last time they'd spoken. He'd tried to call her since, at least a couple of times. He'd written, and she'd never replied. He felt a residual heat creep across his neck.

"Hello?" Martha, soft-voiced in the telephone like a sparrow perched on his shoulder, or a part of himself.

Famke couldn't speak for a moment, and then all emotion came at once and all he could say was: "Where are you?"

Martha hummed a little laugh. "But you called me at home! Where are you?"

"I'm in Danver. I'm still here. But listen, Martha – listen – I'm coming home!"

A rush of static quivered in the line, tangling her reply into an enigma of buzzes and beeps.

"- Crujo?"

"I didn't see him. He's – he's not in Danver and, well, I can't wait here for ever. My bed's about a foot too short. It's too cold. And Martha –" Famke stroked his face. "Well, I'll tell you when I see you."

He felt a sudden urge to tell her a hundred useless things, and then static flooded the wires once more. When it had cleared the line was dead, and Famke found himself booming at the startled café owner instead, "I've missed you!"

He sprung for a taxi to Grand Central Station, and found himself whistling once more while the avenue slid past in a thin mush of melting ice. Dirty sunlight washed the streets, the salted tang of the coast nurtured caramel sweet by vendors at every corner. Famke beamed at his new face hanging in the rear view mirror, and wondered how the Hylanda's door was holding up.

The station was a repository of lost people, or late people, or folk just rushing ever onwards. Famke bought a coffee and a bread roll and wandered between the colonnades checking departure boards. He helped an old man lift his suitcase across the barrier, and then spent considerable time refusing his money. In the end it was simpler to pocket the coins and tip his hat as he'd seen the porters do.

He joined the queue for the ticket office, and regained his minutes by filling out the yellow State travel permit before reaching the counter, carefully printing his name and next of kin.

It was only when he had his ticket that he discovered the deception. He'd put the ticket in his wallet beside the hotel receipt and the tattooed bank note, only to find Marcel had merely scribbled down the hotel's phone number – which anyway was on the receipt. Famke stood for a moment, eyes stinging once more, and then he folded the 50 Mark note reverently and placed it back in his wallet.

He bought a newspaper and scanned the stories. Train crash in Maden. Government corruption. Twenty percent off thermals at some national chain. In Belton, a small boy had slipped through the railings of a third-floor balcony and had landed unhurt and on his feet. The story made the funnies on page 4 because the boy had been wearing a pair of Zeus Wings snow boots. Page 6: ten percent off Zeus Wings.

Famke twisted the newspaper into a tube and jammed it in the railings. He thought about the crash in Maden, and had the sudden conviction to call Martha. His train was just pulling into its concrete berth when he turned and raced through the concourse, Arctic coat flapping ridiculously against his knees.

He'd spent the last of his change on the newspaper and tried to break the fifty at the kiosk – buying the same edition – but the newsagent shook his head balefully: "I can't change that!"

The choice was between the queue for the rest rooms and the ticket office. Famke joined the latter, sweating once more inside his furs. He slapped the note on the counter hard enough to set his chins wobbling.

"Ticket for the next train!"

The man at the counter sighed from behind a cravat.

"Where to?"

"Anywhere!"

The man bristled. His gaze swept past Famke and surveyed the hall for an officer of the law.

"Maden," Famke interjected. "I'm going to Maden."

"You can't go to Maden." He seemed shocked at Famke's callousness. "The line's closed."

A bell rang in the distance, followed by the shriek of a whistle. They echoed across the hall, rebounding and twisting together until it seemed as though all the trains were rushing away.

"Cradensk, then. Give me a ticket to Cradensk!" And then, in a moment of inspiration, "My wife just went into labour!"

The ticket seller rolled his eyes but filled out the paperwork. The remainder of the transaction was completed in silence.

Famke called Martha twice. The first time he let it ring until his ear was hot, and then he slammed the receiver down and immediately dialled again. A guard had appeared at the mouth of the platform, flag clamped under his arm. Famke heard the click. He heard Martha's voice – she sounded out of breath – and then the guard started to lower the barrier.

Famke dropped the receiver and ran. They watched him go – other lost people, late people, folk rushing on. They moved out of his way and he bounced past in a shimmer of fur and flesh.

To Famke, it ertainly *felt* like running. Relatively, it was more a hasty trot. He was still halfway across the concourse when the yellow barrier bounced in its cradle and snapped into place. He stopped and fought for breath. The whistle screamed. Famke puffed his cheeks and watched the train leave without him.

He found a bench and sat jingling the change in his pockets. He'd missed his train and suddenly the afternoon had opened up, cavernous. He could worry about it, he realised, but he was in a train station and, for a man in need of a train, where better to wait? He flipped a coin in his pocket, and wondered which side it showed.

He could wait for the next train. He could wait for any of a hundred trains that would depart between now and night, speeding across the plains in as many directions like marbles in a bowl. He could go to Cradensk. Why, he could go back to the hotel and think it over in the morning.

It struck him that a man could play at many things. Chamber maid. Porter. Who was ever just one thing, with certainty and die-cut precision, between morning and night? A job was just a role one wore during office hours, after all, and not a prediction. Hired Assassin. Chief Medical Officer. And husband?

He thought about Martha and grew sad. He sat for so long in quiet contemplation that someone fetched a guard, and the guard asked him if he was quite all right.

"I missed my train," Famke said. He stretched, rousing nesting pigeons into flight. They circled and wheeled beneath the arched roof as if for show. "Silly things. They could fly free but they stay here, in the dirt and the dark. I wonder why?"

The guard snapped his fingers for Famke's travel permit, lingering over the ink in a most mistrustful manner.

"Dirty? Here?" he sniffed. "Where do you think you are?"

He handed the pass back with miserly grace. When Famke reached for it, the coin jumped from his pocket like a totem and landed on the ground between them. They stared at it surprise.

"It's heads," Famke said.

"It's heads," said the guard. He drummed his fingers against his temple and left giving significant glances to the travellers he passed, each of whom looked the more lost for this secret information.

Famke sat without moving for a while, his thoughts over-taking even the trains and speeding on elsewhere.

He sighed and returned to himself. He unzipped the Arctic coat and unfurled his legs. The coin had landed with its bronzed face winking in the gaslight. A decision had been made. He had all the time in the world.

Each Day, the Sun

The electricity had gone during the night, and in the morning the fan above their bed was like a starfish after the tide. Black flies roosting in the rafters; salt water in the crease of her neck. Isabel tutted and rolled over to tell Cora, but she was just lying there, empty gaze fixed on the ceiling. She looked dull in the dawn, arteries a long way from the reach of the sun. The remembrance of warmth lingered on her skin.

"Coraluna?"

No reply. No stir. No discernible movement.

This was the dead game – they'd played it as girls, biting back laughter in the dark and stealing the thin sheets from each other. They'd kicked and rolled with cichlid grace – once.

Isabel sat up, anger crying out in an ache deep down in twisted bones, in the diffidence of muscle made to bend and work at this early hour. She pinched Cora's hand and the doughy skin stayed peaked. "Are you being lazy? Lazy bones. Get up."

Black dress hanging on the back of the door.

Empty shoes with their patchwork of cardboard in the soles.

Dust on the dresser they shared, the mirror angling to catch the morning.

Isabel held her sister's hand. There seemed nothing more to say.

By noon the colour had come back into Cora's cheeks but still she lay there, oddly angular.

Isabel searched the dresser, fingers falling over wooden beads and linen thread. A metal comb knotted with grey hair. Lacquer boxes and their secret luxuries: a pebble, a clotted pot of rouge, pressed flowers. Her hand closed on a rosette of crumpled notes – barely enough for a bus ride let alone a doctor. *What can they do? Send us away?*

"I'm not going." Cora's fingers plucked at the sheets. "I'm an old woman. Leave me in peace."

They took the bus, jammed together on plastic seats and the voice of the hills calling through the window bars.

The land rolled by, a blur of dust and parched rock. Blank sky greedy on the horizon, with just the shape of condors wheeling above the crags. There were hawkers in straw hats and leather sandals, and shrines by the side of the road, their garlands marking the limits of the land they knew as it passed under the wheels and was gone.

The road unwound through the hills and the air grew thick with the hum of passing trucks and their ziggurats of timber. Solitary houses clustered together and formed streets, then piles of gaudy apartment blocks with their painted faces turned to the sun.

Here there were wooden stalls selling packets of fried almonds and frosted bottles of beer, but Isabel had brought home-baked bread, flat and flaky and peppered with seeds. She broke it in half but Cora shook her head, eyes fixed on the seat in front – she didn't want to see this new place. They sat without speaking, the monstrous noise of the bus multiplying as other traffic joined the procession, and all of them swept onwards.

The hospital waiting hall was a cavernous, concrete space larger than the bus station. It was crammed with folk in their best cotton, sweating in the airless room. Isabel gave the empty seat to Cora and stood fanning them both with official forms: vacant spaces for this and that – a dreadful clamouring to write the past.

"Look at this, Cora. They want our life story!"

Isabel had twisted and piled her sister's hair into a heavy knot that morning. Flattened by the heat and the low roof of the bus it had collapsed, like the sorry symptom of a broken neck. Cora's arm was cool to the touch and she sat unmoving, not listening, her face an impassive almond shell. She chewed a word and finally spat it out: "Malena."

The name was a relic, hidden from daylight for twenty years, perhaps more. Isabel watched beads of sweat line-up along Cora's lip, and then the older woman turned to her and said with spite: "Malena," and finally Isabel followed her gaze.

To look just then was a strange thing: like seeing the outline of a body and waiting for remembrance of flesh. A yellow dress. Ragged curls. Middle age lay in the soft creases of the face, but still Isabel could see the girl they had known as Malena. She was sitting behind a large desk at the end of the hall, head bent as she divided stacks of paper between cardboard folders.

Isabel started up from her chair – and then Cora's hand clamped around hers.

"Don't be a fool. Come. We're leaving."

"We're not leaving. She's our people!"

"We don't even know her people."

"She's from our place. She can help us."

Cora danced the hem of her dress. She sat regally, jewels of sweat on her brow, elegant under her collapsed tower of hair:

"I'd rather die." She'd built a story for herself; had pulled it about her like a winding sheet.

Isabel pushed past, hips creaking against chairs and indignation. "Then die," she replied, and turning away brought to mind things that once had happened, in some fashion – or had not, and never were.

~

There had been fireworks that night.

Even then they were old, walking slowly, arm in arm. It was evening but still warm, the air cloying and steam rising out of the ground.

"Like spirits!" Isabel shivered.

Coraluna tutted and flexed her twisted fingers. Arthritis was a text in her bones, warped and unreadable. Isabel took her hand and she let her rub out the pain, feeling the catch of calluses against her own.

The stalls on the main street had their wooden fronts propped open, lanterns swinging from the poles. The horses had been moved on, but the road still smelled of them, of their excrement mixed with spice and perfume carried on the breeze. A band walked ahead of the crowd, two tin trumpets passing a melody between themselves, singing out in joy for one boy, one girl.

Isabel peered between the rows of people and found the bride under her embroidered headscarf, cheeks blushed by naked flame and excitement for the unknown night.

Coraluna's face was a crow's profile in the dark. "She won't look so sweet after he's had her sister," she whispered.

Night erased Isabel's disapproval, yet left behind a sharpness; a sadness laid heavy in her bones. Cora saw it and said, "So what? So they choose each other for this night, for all nights, until they tire of each other. Choosing is the most they can hope for." She butted the hip beside her and they both laughed, a secret mirth in the sea of joy.

The groom's cousins had arranged fireworks, sending rockets crashing into the sky with whistling ribbons and flame. Boys leaped and danced around the gunpowder – ghosts among smoke – while the crowd cried out as the fire ebbed and then reared up.

They were already turning away. The crowd drifted, joy dissipating after all that splendour – carried home by some, discarded by others among stale cake and horse shit.

The sisters moved slowly, feet dragging on the streets their mother had walked. They nodded at this neighbour, ignored that one, and stopped to fill their kerchiefs with the fried pastries doled out by the bride.

"Bless you, Doma Ernesto!" they called, and the bride blushed under the weight of her newness.

"All happiness!" Coraluna cried out, and watched her sister's face like a shrewd bird.

The bride was young but she caught the edge of the laughter and held herself rigid. But what could she say to two old women of such poverty, of such standing?

"The stray dog has a nose for good fortune," she finally replied, and they stared at her in surprise. She nodded past them, at the child watching from the shadows – a scrawny infant, thin under her dirty dress, brown curls a hazy aureole of tangles and lice.

"You've found a friend," Isabel teased Cora when the girl followed them later. Cora spat her pasticche into her hand, moonlight and crumbs between her crooked teeth.

"The doma needs to learn to cook." She stretched her hand into the blackness behind them. "Come! You're hungry; you'll like this."

There was a scuffle of footsteps, and the girl ran into the night and was gone. The sisters looked at each other in amusement.

"Strange thing," Isabel murmured. "Whose child is she?"

Coraluna tipped her pastries onto the street: flecks of meat among the gravel; oil drops on dust.

"Not ours," she said. "Not ours."

Coraluna was threading wooden beads onto sharp wire. She'd been fast, once, threading 30 or 40 bracelets in one morning, hawking them off between noon and nightfall on the mountain road. Now her fingers were thick and twisted she made less and sold little – as though trinkets may only be traded by the young.

Isabel, pouring a pail of water into the drain in front of the house, felt herself scrutinized. She followed the airless touch of intuition across the dirt-paved street and its gathered pigs and there, half hidden by a wall, was the girl again. The child watched her impassively.

"Ai!" Isabel beckoned.

The girl regarded her in an off-hand way, then vanished among the gutters. Isabel shrugged, but later she said happily, "Your friend is back!"

"Which friend?"

Visitors were rare. If people came, might not these women ask for something? Some expectation of distant bloodline, some charity? But the sisters kept their own house; they fed and clothed themselves. Every day, the sun. Every night, the moon.

"That stray dog from the wedding."

"That girl? Why has she come here? We can't feed her."

Isabel untied a cloth bundle – skirts with hanging pockets; bodices ripped from their sleeves. This was why people came, if they came as far as the veranda.

"Are you listening?" Coraluna demanded.

Each thing she mended Isabel turned inside out and sliced a thin strip from the lining or an open hem: fragments too small to be missed, and which she tucked away in a bag at her feet.

"If God meant you to have children, he'd have given you one of your own." Cora's eyebrows rose on her forehead and the devil bridged the gap. "He would have sent you a man in the first place."

Isabel bent her head. She didn't want to ruin the blouse, didn't want to sacrifice the strip. She sensed the blur of Cora's hands, of beads slipping onto thin wire. Each bead fell with a tut, like keys on a chain, like constriction. Isabel was on her feet; a slow rising, summoned. She'd tamped the blouse into a cannonball and flung it, hard, into her sister's face.

"There!" her thin voice like a child's, "soak up some of your bile —" and she summoned vile words about cursed women and dogs in the street, and all the world of misfortune and unfairness. She slammed the door as she left, but the only response that followed was the growl of beads rolling beneath the chairs.

By evening the unpleasantness had evaporated along with the drain water. The sisters sat down to eat with the doors open. The sky was grey-faced for the end of summer, for the coming of rains and frost.

"She's still out there. I wonder where she lives? Maybe she's an orphan."

"She's a con artist."

Isabel laughed.

"She's a baby!"

"This is the new world," said Cora. "You don't know how people are these days."

Isabel surveyed the room.

"What can she steal from us? Poverty? Lord, let us be quick to share it should the chance come along!"

Cora fixed her eyes on her sister. "Alright. But this was your idea. Remember that."

She stacked the day's bread in both hands and sailed out of the room with missionary zeal.

Moments later she returned and threw the loaf on its platter:

"Stupid thing needs an invitation!"

**

Each year a circus had passed through the deadlands. It was a ragged collection of lean folk and desperadoes, and animals both real and stuffed, and a man with a second, stunted head growing out of his neck. They set up camp on the side of the road and walked into town, the man with two heads at the front of the procession. He kept his second head under a purple hood.

All of them were shouting and singing, telling jokes and tumbling; drawing the townsfolk out from the fields where they slept and worked, pulling them like a gathered skirt across the dust bowl. They looped around the landscape, a caravan shifting against the sky and climbing between boulders. They spilled across the high plains, along gravel shards that, one day, would resettle into a pan-American highway blistered onto the land.

There, by the road that did not yet exist, the circus pinwheeled under the gaze of falcons and vultures, throwing down its load among open fires and metal pots of boiling corn, while acrobats tumbled like wooden jacks cast beneath the sun.

They told stories, some never heard before and unimaginable in their fiction, and the townspeople shook their heads, and some of them tutted and rolled their eyes. The man with the second head pulled off his purple hood with great flourish, and this always raised a gasp – but it was the bear that caused the most excitement.

"Fight him!" cried the ringmaster, his arms spread before him, his second head sleeping on his shoulder. "The man who beats him takes our money!" He meant the money the people had paid to watch the show, and all the tumbling and the card games, but he didn't say that most of it was already hidden away inside his shirt.

Coraluna and Isabel were still girls then, Cora's hair long in woven knots. She gripped her sister in excitement but Isabel stood biting her fingers. Both were thinking of the bear fight, watching the tight noose of people gathering in the distance.

"Come," Cora said, but Isabel shook her head.

"I don't want to see the bear."

Cora pinched the thin skin at the nape of the child's neck. "Come!" she cried.

The bear was a beast only by species. The circus folk kept him on a chain and mostly he was lethargic and niggardly furred. They poured water on him and tugged him onto his back legs, and then he stood and looked at them all like a totem swaying in the thin air.

The first man to fight jumped and skipped like he was dancing, and everyone roared with laughter. He ran up under the bear and pushed him, and the bear came down on all fours. It shook its muzzle in confusion and everyone cheered and the man was given a coin. He wanted to go on, but the showman said his turn was over.

"Who's next?" he shouted, both heads leering at the crowd. "Who's brave enough to fight the bear?"

Cora, peering through the circle of faces, found Estovan. He grinned at her and made arm-show that he would be next, even though he was just a boy under his stringy muscles. When he was manhandled out of line he spat in disgust. Cora watched him lope across the field, waiting for him to turn even as he disappeared among the gamblers.

Isabel watched the fight but wouldn't cheer and cry out like the others. She stood without speaking, eyes fixed somewhere in the unformed distance, swaying along to some unheard tune. Cora touched her, and she didn't stir. The wind whipped through the crowd like a breath, and with it came daring – and so Cora crept away. She looped around the knot of spectators, disappearing between the wagons and cooking pits.

The bear fight went on into the evening and five or six men went home victorious, and others who hadn't built the nerve to fight went home empty-handed, but saying how tomorrow, and tomorrow, and tomorrow, they would bring down the bear in a way never yet seen.

The circus folded itself up, tables dismantled and packed away along with the pots and bottles. The people dispersed, their shadows sinking back into the mountains from which they were born. Families and loners and orphans and all were wending their way under starlight. Some of them, as they passed, called out but Isabel, spinning in the dark and her hair whipped this way and that, wouldn't reply. She flailed against the night, unable to go, or stay, only to turn in circles. Then Cora, like a white shroud walking, came striding out of the darkness.

"Where have you been! I've been looking everywhere." She caught Isabel by the shoulder and slapped her. "Why don't you pay any mind to where you go?"

Then the two of them were tipping and tumbling along the stone road, cheeks burned in the wind and both of them swallowed by the end of day. Isabel also burned with resentment, gathering together words for one day not yet made.

After a while Cora murmured, "Don't tell mother you got lost, will you?"

She moved under the moonlight, boiling with innocent memory and the skin at the neck of her blouse still warm, grazed by two playing cards pierced together and pinned in place. It was intent. It was promise. It was all warm currency now.

So the circus came and went, as it did each year, until its last ever day, when the rains had come early and the dust bowl was a muddy arena. This year the people sat on wooden benches and upturned boxes, grime at their feet and water overhead.

The circus had acquired a new performer, a reedy girl who sang a high, forlorn song about birds lost in the mountains and Coraluna cried to hear it.

"What are you crying for?" Isabel wanted reason to cry too, but Coraluna wouldn't say. She had started tying her plaits on top of her head, reaching for womanhood one pin at a time. "Are you thinking about –"

"Oh shush!"

By the time the bear was presented the sky was dark, and torches had been lit around the camp. It was like a great wedding, with music and dancing, and the shape of the mountains behind them, and the wind undecided in its coming and going.

The bear had grown some, though it looked thinner for it – sunken in the face and belly, and somehow lacking overall.

"Fight him!" cried the man with two heads, although this year he didn't remove his purple hood and wouldn't say why, though the people had their own speculation. "The man who beats him takes our money!" – but only he and his cronies knew where the sum of it was hidden.

The first man who came forward had an easy job. The bear lurched like it was drunk, moored in place by the chain around its neck and glaring through the rain. At the first blow it fell into the mud and lay there, and everyone held their breath thinking that this year, the prize would be won. The man with two heads tugged on the chain, but still the bear lay in the dirt.

A light breeze moved through its damp fur. The bear shuffled to its feet and then sat on its hind legs like a grandmother, and the crowd roared.

The man with two heads thought for a while, and then he said, "Who's next? Who can win the last fight of the evening?"

There was muttering from the crowd, then, because it seemed unfair; a double-cross.

Several men pushed and jostled to be the last to fight, but it was Estovan who broke through the ring of tangled arms. He turned to the crowd and bowed, the rain clinging to his bare chest. His black hair was like a silk rag on his head. In the downpour he seemed oiled and taut, firelight glistening across his new down.

The bear wouldn't stand and the man with two heads beat it with a stick until it reared up on its hind legs, all the time shaking its head in a dazed way.

Isabel bit her fingers. "If I were the bear I'd have snapped the chain and run away into the hills," but she looked at the chain coiled along the ground and felt unsure.

Estovan jumped and paraded in front of the bear, while the crowd shouted encouragement and the man with two heads watched with a smirk on his true face. Cora clenched her fists and turned away, staring out at the garlands of baked corn, at ribbons of meat charred and black in their skins.

The fighter slipped in the mud and the crowd gasped. Then he found his hold and his daring: he pranced in front of the bear and smacked its muzzle with his fist. The bear came down on all fours.

"Stand up and fight, you coward!" cried the man with two heads, and his associate yanked its chain until the bear reared up once more. The associate aimed a kick at the bear, too, but the ringmaster shook his working head.

Estovan leaned in for the fight, weaving away from the claws and calling out obscenities that no one could understand. The crowd yelled and their cheers carried him forward: he wrapped his arms around the bear's chest.

The man with two heads started up and shouted at his associate, who picked up a stick and started hitting the bear from behind. The bear flung its arms in the air and then it toppled forward

– claws skittering across the mud – both man and bear wrapped in one embrace. They fell and lay there for a moment, and then the bear shuddered and tried to stand but couldn't.

The show was ended then, on account of Estovan being dead under the bear's accidental muzzle and claws. The man with the two heads had all the men and women of the circus stand in front of the body. "Send them home!" he was shouting from under his wet moustache, though he let the boy's father stay and showed him and the family some kindness.

Coraluna had screamed when the bear fell, turning her face once more into the darkness. Now she wrapped her fingers around her sister's wrist like a bracelet.

"Come," she whispered, "we should leave," and they both sat there till they were frozen in the black night.

"Do you ... want to go to Estovan?"

Coraluna didn't reply. She gazed at the family members being herded away – they formed an impenetrable circle in the low light. She looked, too, at the girl who had promised herself to Estovan; his token around her neck on a second-hand chain.

"Come. We should leave," and they walked across the field holding onto each other.

Isabel looked over her shoulder as they left, finding it strange that now they showed the bear some kindness – that now, when they wanted it to stand, they did so with fruit.

**

There were palm fruits on the veranda, and limes, and tiny melons with skins the colour and texture of russet pumpkin. Isabel said it would spoil in the heat.

"None of these things are sweet. Children like sweet things."

Coraluna rolled her eyes.

"What do you know about children?" She placed the platters behind the grill which separated the house from the heat of the garden; arrangements of low-hanging fruit for small hands.

One doma passing a bundle of dresses through the railings had peered at the fruit in surprise, and then into Isabel's face.

"Are you setting up shop?" She'd pressed her face against the grill and opened her eyes wide, like an owl before it eats the young of lesser birds.

This particular doma was cheap. She wore the seams on her clothes so narrow that there was no allowance. One skirt had a finger-long tear above the hem. Isabel stabbed it with her needle. The hole couldn't just be sewn up, or the hem would be ragged, yet she'd given nothing to patch it.

Isabel remembered the face pressed against the grill and sliced at the hem. Women like the doma obsessed over details. She'd go through all these clothes afterwards and inspect the seams with her owl eyes, and she wouldn't even notice the skirt was two inches shorter. And so what if she did?

"How else did you expect me to patch your carelessness?" Isabel asked the memory of the doma. "Do you think I'm made of linen?" She held out her wrist. "Here. Take it from here!"

"Who are you talking to?" Cora came into the room slowly, uneven on her hips.

Isabel pulled the scissors faster, fibres flying into the air. "How many days do you plan on displaying all our fruit like this?"

Cora sat and pulled the tray of beads into her lap. She shrugged and danced the threads like a puppet show.

"Why do you bother stealing those scraps? Why not just fix the dresses and be done with it? Charge more."

"You never understand anything."

"No, of course. I'm just an old woman." And she bowed her head in deference.

By the end of the week the autumn flies had meddled with the plump flesh. The whole house smelled sour.

"I told you this would happen."

The sisters stood with their heads bowed over the browning harvest.

"Make ice-cream."

"You hate ice-cream. And you picked all sour fruit. Even the neighbour's children wouldn't steal it."

"Then throw it in the gutter for the pigs," Cora said.

It was unthinkable, and so Isabel made the ice-cream. They ate it like a punishment supper, and, with each mouthful, Cora puckered her lips and swore.

It wasn't the rotting fruit, or the ice-cream addling in the parlour, or even the bracelets strung along the window grills. The girl came of her own volition and, one morning, was sitting on the veranda with her feet in Isabel's slippers.

The sisters hid inside, pretending they hadn't noticed.

"Let's have another breakfast," whispered Isabel, reaching for a plate of pancakes still warm in their grease.

"She's not hungry," Cora said stoutly. "She didn't want any fruit."

"No one wanted the fruit."

"You don't know anything about children."

"You know half as much."

Cora opened the door and smiled into the sky as though the sun had come that morning as a personal favour. And then, as though a child on the doorstep were a common thing, picked up a half-strung bracelet and sat wordlessly beside the girl. She clanked each bead down and shook the string, blue stones blinking in the sunlight. Then she picked up the wire and looped it back and forth. Periodically she stopped and jangled the beads, the melody dropping through its scale as the wire tightened its grip.

Isabel watched them from the kitchen window, shadows falling across her face in dark welts. The girls' head was tipped at an angle of fascination, hair like a torn feather pillow.

"Well!" Isabel tutted. What did Cora know about children? Nothing. And yet it was enough. She turned away and clicked the gas burner sitting on its stone base. Methane curled between the shelves and the photos of their parents pinned to the wall.

"Well!"

The kitchen was oppressive, but the back yard was too hot. The day was dull, and she wasn't wanted. She sliced tomatoes and salted them. She listened to the chickens arguing in the yard.

The front of the house was silent and she crept to the window again and peeped. The two of them were still there, like an ant and its shadow. Ridiculous.

She ate lunch alone, folding pancake doilies around stewed pork. She found a black and armoured millipede at the back of the pantry, and crushed it with her finger.

Afternoon was stealing onto the veranda by the time Cora came inside. She smacked her lips hungrily.

"Well?" Isabel's face was pinched.

Coraluna tipped the covers from the empty pots slowly, delicately. Outside the chickens shrieked and fussed, racing each other in their womb of dry dirt.

"Idle hands built the devil's playground," Cora answered at last.

"That's stupid. If the hands were lazy they wouldn't have built anything."

"What's for lunch?" Cora crowed. "I've worked up an appetite!"

Isabel folded her hands, holding each nail prisoner.

"What happened?"

Cora laughed and held up an arm decked in blue-bead finery.

"Look! Aren't they awful! But she can learn."

Isabel's face grew hot.

"You can't be thinking to sell them."

"And why not? This isn't a mission school. It's a reasonable trade for my time."

"Who asked for your time?" Isabel would have stood, but the afternoon was weighty overhead.

"Malena did. When she followed me home from the wedding. Yes, she followed me! You said so yourself."

"Malena? Her name is Malena?"

"That's what I've decided to call her," Cora's voice crept out from the pantry. "Don't you think she looks just like her? And Isabel? Where's our lunch?"

Isabel stayed silent. Outside the chickens screamed, each vying for the victory of the last pancake.

If the girl had a name of her own, she didn't reveal it. She sat with Coraluna and was always silent at first, gentle so as not to break the morning. Strings of blue beads accumulated on the table behind the door, and along the window sills. At first they were crooked and loose, and later taut and glistening with intricate pattern. Whether they were better than Coraluna's was a matter of debate never definitively answered.

"But what do you talk about?" Isabel wanted to know. The sisters were watching evening roll in and drinking beer from brown bottles. Cora's hand was in hers, curled and stiff at the day's end.

"The state of the national economy. What do children talk about? Little things. Nothing things."

Isabel set her mouth with lemon shrillness.

"Well, it's like this. When she comes in the morning, I open the door. We see each other, but we don't say anything. No 'good morning'. We just sit and start working. Only after a little while we start talking – like a conversation we were already having."

Isabel was incredulous. "Conversation about what?"

"Just as I say. Little things. Nothing things. She asks questions – all kinds of questions. You couldn't imagine them!"

Isabel rolled her eyes.

"She asked why my hands look this way. Whether it's painful. Do the beads come from trees – do we pluck them like fruit!"

"And what did you tell her?"

Evening was hard against the window, the moon smiling behind clouds and Coraluna laughing into the neck of the bottle.

"Why don't you ask her yourself? Always hiding in the kitchen. Why all the questions and jealousy? Nobody asked you to stay away."

"What about her family? She won't eat with us. She must have family."

They watched a lizard come to life on the wall, as though their looking had disturbed it. It scuttled away behind a cabinet.

Cora drank deeply before replying. "Ah. I've never thought to ask."

"How old are you now, old woman?"

Isabel asked every year. Cora merely bowed, gracious in her hatred of show and pomp and birthdays.

The day was dry, a kind of barrenness which settled against the walls and the grain of the floorboards. Outside the dirt track was desiccated, cracked veins split open and waiting for the rains.

There would be no birthday feast, but for breakfast Isabel stewed tomatoes till they were sour in their skins, because she liked to see the old woman smack her lips. It seemed impossible that anything could be as sharp as Coraluna, but here it was on a platter.

"Do you think that people are like the weather?" Isabel waited for Cora to frown. Cora was of a very scientific mind.

"What weather? What people?"

Isabel drew a bow in the sauce with her finger.

"Maybe people born under the sun are hot-headed. Fiery. Or cold-hearted, those winter children. Like that."

"Well now! And what was the weather for me, when I was born? What do you imagine?"

Each shrewdly appraised the other.

"Well ..." Isabel was thoughtful. "Your birthday falls right between autumn and winter. Weighty weather, like today. Portentous. Yes. I think the day you were born, there was a storm brewing." Cora laughed in delight. "And me?" Isabel wanted to know.

"You were born in summer, and so you are."

"You think I'm hot-headed?"

"You're inevitable. And irritating in excess."

A summer bird called out a farewell from the garden.

"Do you ever think about mother?"

Cora shrugged. "Do you?"

"I don't know. Yes."

Cora leaned forward in her chair.

"What things?"

Isabel blushed first, and then she said: "I see her standing in the corner of the room folding sheets. I hear her saying all those things. How we should live. How we should eat. What was good, or not good. How to cook pasticche so the cases don't crack." She paused. "I miss being someone's child, the jewel more precious than anything."

There was silence, and stillness. Even the birds had done with song for the day. Cora flung her spoon on the table.

"Thank you for this heart-warming recollection! If you were to make every day so cheerful I don't know how I could contain the joy of it."

"Then don't ask me again," Isabel snapped, and shut herself in the kitchen.

That afternoon Cora worked at something secret, hunting through cupboards and overturning boxes.

"What are you looking for?"

Cora wouldn't say. She pressed her lips, and left the drawers hanging out on their tongues. Eventually she reappeared from the cupboard clasping a tarnished silver cuff. Dark bubbles had sprouted along its surface and the delicate chain-work detail had snapped away some time ago, and yet it held its shape and lustre.

Isabel grabbed for it. "But that was mother's!" She turned the bracelet in her hand like a wonder. "You made such a fuss about it. You wanted it. You took it. And you've never even looked at it, all these years! You've ruined it." She threw it on the bed and it rolled off and fell between them.

"Don't be so dramatic." Cora wiped the bracelet on her skirt. "I'll polish it. You'll never know the difference."

"You're giving it to me now? After all this time? I begged you for it then. It's too late now."

"I'm not giving it to you. What do you want with it? You have all your memories of folding laundry. No, you said Malena shouldn't work for nothing. I'll give it to her."

Isabel chewed her lip, a scarlet flush running up her neck.

"But it's ridiculous. You can't give just one like that. They're always worn in pairs. And besides, it's so large. It'll fall right off her arm!"

Cora cast a meaningful glance at her sister. "She is very slender, it's true. But I'll make it fit, why not?"

"Why not? Why not?" Isabel twisted her mouth, but was unable to say further than that.

By evening the silver cuff was a gleaming crescent on the shelf. Coraluna worked at her trinkets once more, head cocked as though following a tune in the tumble of beads.

"I wonder where she is," Isabel murmured. "She comes every day." She was planted in the bedroom doorway, framed against black shadows and nothingness.

"Who?"

Isabel smiled into the corner of the room and pulled something from behind her back. "Here," she said. "I made it for you."

They stared at the bundle, identical in the creases of their eyes.

Cora turned it over and shook it out across the table. It was a muddy patchwork of fabric – old pockets and skirt hems and shoulder seams and collars, all furrowed together with broad new stitches. A blanket, warm in its lining, with a neat, silk-edged border. It was functional – if without finer grace.

"I made it for you."

"Why?"

Isabel patted away some imagined dust. "Why not?"

Cora glanced into her bead box.

"You always let your heart get the better of your sense. What do I need with another blanket? We can get a decent price for this." Beads fell along her wire once more.

"I won't sell it! I made it for you."

"You could have made three blankets out of this. You still can."

Isabel smoothed the covers hanging on the backs of the chairs. She straightened a jug. She wiped the dust from the table with the palm of her hand.

"If it's a hard winter, won't you be in pain? Won't your fingers be too stiff to work? Won't mine? Don't you know why I made it?"

"You made it because we're old. But you and I, we've grown old making do with what we have. So what? Cut it, girl. I'll take it with me tomorrow, or the day after. Cut it." She looked up. "Or I will."

Isabel turned to the window. "Don't you know?"

Evening hung heavy, with no hint of reply. Isabel fetched the shears.

Malena came the following day, eyes puffy in her caramel face. She looked unexpectedly clean; newly bathed, and with a fresh patch on her dress.

"You didn't come yesterday," Cora said, watching her out of the corner of her eyes. It was a white dress, already grubby at the hem, its lace trim coming away at the back.

"Don't think I was sitting here waiting for you!" she grumbled to the girl's broad smile. "But you could have come to say you weren't coming. Couldn't you?"

The girl swung her legs under her dress, back and forth like a song. They were sitting on the veranda, facing the everyday street as though some aspect of it had been previously missed. Pigs rolling in the dirt, dusty in their black skins; the concrete trough brimming with rain water – it was none of it new now.

Cora yawned. "I found something. You might like it."

She displayed the silver cuff, angling it to catch the light and watching the child's gaze move in time to the sway. Finally she placed it on the girl's arm, pinching the soft metal until it sighed and closed.

"What were you doing yesterday?" but the girl was distracted, turning her wrist this way and that, bouncing sunlight across the floor. Cora watched the tiny head lost behind all those tangles.

"Do you like it?"

The head nodded. "Like it," she sang.

"It was our mother's. I polished it for you, but it's so very old. You must take care of it. It would be a terrible thing if you lost it, or broke it."

The girl gave a quick nod and then looked up expectantly. Cora frowned.

"There were two, once. The other was lost a long time ago. Anyway, why should you care?" She plucked at the girl's dress. "Is one bracelet not enough for such finery?"

Malena stood and presented herself solemnly to be inspected, and pushed her hair behind her shoulders. It was a strange, womanly movement – disconcerting, somehow.

"Very nice," Cora heard herself saying, and then, once more: "What were you doing yesterday?"

"My sister's wedding. Do you know my sister?" The girl gave a sudden, darting movement, stepping forward to squeeze the old woman's cheeks between her hands. It was a queer thing – it brought to mind the image of other women, of grandmothers, mothers, aunts. Cora unpeeled the hands.

"I didn't know you had a sister. Do you have a large family? How many sisters, brothers?"

"Lots," the girl said, and performed a twirl in the shadow of the grill. She stopped and inspected the bracelet again. "But two aren't here any more."

"How many of you are there?"

The girl held up both hands.

"So you're not an urchin at all."

Malena held her skirt out to the side and took a small step as though waiting for the band. The arm bearing the bracelet was held aloft – and Coraluna swooped down and grabbed it. The bracelet tore away, leaving a bright red twin in its wake.

The girl stood frozen, tangles trembling in the breeze.

"How many bracelets do you have?" Coraluna's voice ricocheted against the railings. "How many did you wear last night? You won't need another. And you needn't think about taking this one and giving it away, either!"

No reply. No stir. No discernible movement.

Eddies of dust sighed and shifted, a blurred blanket that rose and fell and erased the cracks in the street.

Cora sighed. She turned to the child, staring at her in surprise as though the morning was yet to happen.

"Go home," she spat. "Go home."

There was no coming back from Cora's resolve; it was hard-shelled and bitter, even as they undressed for bed.

"But what did she do?" Isabel asked.

"The girl's a liar! She's a cheat! I told you this from the beginning. I said it was on your head."

"Because she went to a wedding? Because she has a sister? But we knew she wasn't an urchin! Didn't you wonder where she slept at night?"

Cora turned her head on the pillow, a thin plait coiled across her shoulder.

"You are a malicious old woman."

Isabel laughed to hear it. "Is that so?"

"It's exactly so. So the girl visited me. So she sat with me. And you sat in the kitchen and cracked your thumbs and anyway, who asked you to? Better the devil had taken shelter under your wing. Daring to ask me had I thought this or that, when you were the one boiling your head."

Isabel turned away. Night lay against the window sill while the hens crooned the day's news in the sleeping dark. Cora's voice raged on:

"What do you know? You can't understand, you just know your needle and thread. You live between the four walls."

"Where should I live?" Isabel yawned, "on the moon?"

"You couldn't know," Cora said. "You couldn't even have children of your own."

Isabel screwed her eyes shut.

"Oh, to have been blessed with your brood, then."

There was a thin cord of silence between them, and then the fan cut through with its whispered growl.

"I had a child, once."

Isabel stifled a smile against the pillow. "Just one?"

"I had a child, almost. When I was a girl."

Isabel opened her eyes. The room was grey, its paltry furniture waiting and a thin gleam dancing along the crucifix on the wall.

"And where was I?"

There was a small hiss of laughter.

"I don't know, in your mother's apron maybe."

"Where?"

"You were there. But you were a child. What did you know about anything?"

Jesus was falling, it seemed, from his cross, yet forever suspended in gloom.

"How? How did you have a child?"

"The usual way."

"Then who?"

There was movement beside her. She waited for the answer.

"Just."

"Then?"

The reply, when it came, was low: "Then nothing, just as I say. Mother was there. She told me what it was, what had happened. But I already knew what had happened. And then Papa found out and he beat me so hard –"

"– that you couldn't stand for days. Why didn't you tell me what really happened? Even later? I wasn't always a child. Why not?"

"Because my life is not your life."

Isabel stared into the dark, her dull eyes holding the moonlight.

"No," she agreed. "Then why now?"

"Just like that."

They lay without speaking, each remembering their life apart.

"Sometimes I feel heavy. Inside." The words were softly spoken, travelling the years and across the bed sheets. "Isn't it ridiculous? This foolish old woman – I have nothing inside."

"Yes." Isabel felt for the hand beside hers. "Foolish old woman."

Malena's mother, when she came, was a harassed looking woman with yet another baby hoisted on one hip. She was a slight thing, birdlike in her limbs, but when her jumper rode up it revealed a loose canvas of flesh crossed with silvery scars. Behind her the sky was blank and formless, with unending sheets of low cloud. Summer was done, and the ground was wet.

Coraluna thought the woman had come to curse them.

"Why should she curse me?" Isabel was indignant. "I didn't do anything!" But Cora wouldn't come out of the kitchen.

The doma, for her part, wouldn't come in – for shyness, rather than spite – so Isabel went out to the veranda, and the two of them took took tea in quiet awkwardness.

The woman smiled and played her tongue against her teeth. She was still beautiful, Isabel could see, and childish in her manners; she twisted the material of her cotton skirt as she talked. She had some secret grace to her; she was captivating. She'd brought a corn cake, sticky and springy in its metal pot.

"She didn't tell me," the woman was saying. "I heard it from my neighbours, can you imagine?" She laughed, but her face was undecided. "Don't think I asked her to come."

"But what's to mention it? The child came here a few times, why should we begrudge her?" Isabel watched the baby drooping against its mother's shoulder. Not delicious, as babies usually are, it was wan-faced, with a heavy, knowing expression.

"She said she likes coming here and talking with you. Ha – she doesn't have words to spare for us." The woman tutted, and a scowl marred her face. "Of course, if you don't want her any more, you should just say."

Isabel was dumbfounded. "But we like her coming!"

"Ah!" the woman said. A cupboard door creaked inside the house and she glanced around the veranda, seeing diamonds in the rusting grill and the cracks in the floor. "She seems to like coming here! She says you taught her how to make bracelets."

"She learned that from my sister," Isabel said quickly.

The woman looked serious, a maturity coming quickly to her face. "I'm grateful."

"And ... that's why you came?"

"If she's learning a trade of some kind – well, I'm grateful to you."

"And what does the child say?" Cora demanded, materialising in the doorway.

The visitor started up out of her chair, a ferocious blush chasing away the dignity, and the whole ceremony had to be run through again. Here was the cake. Here was the thanks. Here was the laying out of expectation.

"She calls you grandmother," the doma said, and then added tactfully, "she thinks of you both like that."

"Of course, she should come, if she wants. But we'd thought perhaps she'd tired of us." Cora watched the street for a moment. "She left suddenly, the last time she was here."

"Oh?" The doma shifted the baby on her shoulder and shrugged non-committally, her gaze fixed on the dark room beyond. So she hadn't come to curse them after all, Isabel thought. She'd come out of curiosity stronger even than concern.

"I think," Cora said loftily, "she was upset about a bracelet. There was a misunderstanding. The bracelet was my mother's." Her hand went to her skirt pocket and dallied there.

"Bracelet?" The woman dragged her thoughts back to the veranda and the dull day. "Oh – yes, she mentioned something. But upset? No. It was just a bracelet. She was laughing about it."

"Laughing?" Cora's smile was a dagger's blade. Isabel looked away quickly.

"Well, yes." The doma giggled and her hair shuddered in the breeze. "Because there was only one! She thought that was funny."

"Ah!" Coraluna laughed gaily. Her hand returned from its pocket and lay, empty, in her lap. "Then of course, she should come." She hesitated, and Isabel watched the clouds moving slowly across her face. "If she wants to, and of course, if we're not otherwise too busy."

Isabel shuddered in her thin dress. The conversation stalled, and they sat in silence. Eventually the doma nodded, but still her eyes darted this way and that, freezing the shape of the house and its shadows into her remembrance of that day. She turned on the step as she left, her face serious once more.

"I'm glad to know you," she said formally. "Evi thinks very much of you."

For some time afterwards, Coraluna regarded the street while, in her pocket, her fingers tapped a message along the edge of the bracelet.

It was Isabel who spoke first, her voice soft in its surprise.

"So that's the child's name!"

Overhead, morning broke like a revelation.

The following day started with an argument about a dog and, later, Isabel saw it as an omen – as though the day's reckoning must be first mapped out with words.

Franco Pierro was a street dog named for one of the mission school teachers and – like the namesake – was a beast prone to wandering and sticking its nose into other's people's business. He was a yellow, mangy looking thing with an excess of both fur and jowls which gave him an aspect hard to love, and that was unfortunate.

When they could catch him they harnessed his labour to the tiny milling wheel in the yard, to save their mother the trouble. Then he would disappear for days, until some harried homesteader arrived on their doorstep demanding they collect the animal.

Sometimes the dog chose unwisely, and arrived covered in welts – and on one occasion, with part of his tail severed clean away. They'd nursed him, then, wrapping him in blankets and cradling his head. Even their father had wiped the soil from his hands and cooked tiny pancakes, just for Franco Pierro. A few days later, the dog was gone again, roaming free and living the kind of life they could never hope to know.

"Well, Papa was such a wonderful man," Cora said bitterly when the subject arose that morning.

Isabel rifled through her sewing basket before speaking.

"I suppose it was his dog, if anyone's. That dog chose its own affections."

"The only affection that dog knew was in the kitchen. Or from like-minded fools." Her gaze bore down on Isabel, who could only smile weakly.

"But that's how animals are."

"What do you take me for, some kind of half-wit? Of course he was a dog. What did you think, I thought he was a doctor?"

"I mean, so the dog looked for food and sometimes company and there was nothing he could give back except being … that kind of dog."

Coraluna rolled her eyes. "He was a malicious, dirty creature. Do you remember" – she threw her hands in the air – "do you remember, he destroyed my blue dress!"

"You shouldn't have left it on the floor. You were always so untidy. Even mother said –"

"I know what mother said. I haven't lost my memory. Or my brain, as you seem to think." She was implacable, and irritated. But then, thought Isabel, so she always was.

"That dress wasn't destroyed. You wore it for some time afterwards."

"Yes," Cora spat, "but it always stank."

The shadows deepened in the corners of the room. Morning ebbed away into a bright noon, though outside the weeds curled in on themselves. Isabel sighed and threw her lot in with the hopeless.

"Do you care to know what I think?"

"But please! Do tell!"

"You cared for the dog as much as we all did. But you won't forgive him because he came and went as he chose. And now I'm saying it was a long time ago, and he was just a dog."

Cora didn't reply. She worked her lips thin and bit them ragged.

Each remembered the day that Franco Pierro had died. They were grown by then, their oiled plaits thick and black. The dog, meanwhile, had grown grey whiskers, and great bald patches from some infestation, but still he wandered like a paramour.

He'd been gone for days, and yet there was no irate neighbour (or, as one occasion, a furious doma with a dead chicken). Between times, they looked for him. They waited, but he didn't come.

"I didn't care for him," Cora insisted. "He was a rogue."

She'd found him while walking home along the river. It was early in the year, and the grass had grown wild and thickly knotted.

The dog had crawled inside a thorn bush, his split stomach oozing dark fluid. He raised his head when Cora came near and watched as she bent low, pressing her face against the branches. She looked down at him with irritation at first. Flies moved slowly over his body, polite in their patience. His fur was singed, the yellow hair dulled and black. It was unthinkable that someone would do such a thing – Franco Pierro was well known in that place. And even then, to have left him half-finished: it was a cruelty from a low place.

"Come!" Cora stretched out her hand. Franco Pierro regarded her for a moment and then lay his head on the ground. She shook the branches, but they gathered on themselves like a tight cage, impenetrable.

"Come out!" she called again, and clicked her tongue.

The dog watched her awhile and then – as was his way – ignored her.

Cora twined her fingers among the thorns and pulled. The branches danced and sprang back into place.

"Stupid thing. You never come when I call!" She shredded her fingers and the sleeves of her blouse. She tugged at the twines until there was a gap, then pressed her shoulder against the opening. "Come!" she called – but the dog had died, and could never now be roused.

"Even then," Cora recalled, "even then. If I called him, he wouldn't come. Not for scraps or saving. You should have found him. Or Papa, or any one other than me."

"He would have died anyway," Isabel said softly, but Cora shook her head.

"Like that? Like something thrown into the yard for the chickens?"

Isabel pushed her sewing to one side.

"But that's how animals are. He was just a dog. He had his own kind of affection, I suppose." She remembered the wet feel of his nose pushing into her hand, vigorous and insistent as though independent of its owner. "If he came and went, what does that mean other than he could?"

Cora's voice rose taut and clear:

"That is the difference between you and me, girl. You allow any stray to bleed you dry. Sing me more love songs, Isabela Carito Maria, and stay wrong-headed and utterly useless."

On reflection, it seemed to Isabel that it didn't do to be so coy with Coraluna. One ought to come right out and speak the thing that was in the mind or the heart. And, if it lay there trembling like a piglet on a butcher's block – if it couldn't withstand Cora's judgement – why, so be it.

Early evening, and cicadas had gathered in the gloom, the night stretched thin with their percussive hum. Isabel was in the kitchen entreating hot peppers to blacken their skins, so it was Coraluna who answered an unexpected knock at the door.

It was raining, the child standing there with dress and curls soaking, barefoot as a cat. She trailed one finger against the door frame and smiled coyly. Cora's mouth made the shape of a broken vowel, but she planted herself firmly in the doorway.

"Oh, do you deign us with your presence? And just as we eat! Your mother has good timing, to send you to call on paupers in the evening."

Rain ran along the girl's nose and she sniffed it in. "We ate," she said. "What are you eating?"

"What does it have to do with you?"

The girl's grin wavered – but only for a moment.

"What are you doing here?" Cora demanded. "Looking for something else to laugh about with your mother? Or sent to spy out some detail of our home that escaped her attention when she was here? God knows, she looked hard enough. Could she have missed anything?"

The words were more noise than meaning, but they were hard-edged. The girl's smile faded and she stood twisting her foot against the floor. She was caught between staying and going; between childishness and the weight of the world. Her face grew sullen. "Want to make bracelets," she said, and stared up at the old woman.

"Well you can't," Cora hissed. "Because –" and she laid out reason in her mind while her mouth chased its own quarry. "Because you're not wanted."

She slammed the door in the girl's face, hard enough to make the picture frames jump. And then – it could only have been the tiniest portion of a second – the girl started screaming.

Coraluna stood breathing heavily, a sharp pain suddenly lodged deep in her hip. She opened the door fearfully.

"What's this noise?" She was trembling despite herself.

The child was on the floor, writhing and gasping for breath. There was a thin spatter of blood beside her.

"What is it?" Cora cried, "what happened?" But the girl wouldn't answer, rolling over and over as though dousing flames that couldn't be seen.

Cora pulled her close and held her and, slowly, the girl softened and stilled. Cora unfurled the clenched fist and cried out. The very tip of the child's finger – it had been resting against the door when Cora had slammed it – had been sliced clean away. It was a small wound, superficial but for the blood and the noise.

The old woman tore the lace from her collar and wrapped it tightly around the cut. The child sniffed and thrust her head into the old woman's neck. Still the cicadas droned on, mechanical and loveless in their wooing. The child turned her head against the warmth. "Ma," she crooned, and lay there without moving.

Coraluna had held the girl fiercely, their bodies pressed together, soft flesh against old bones. Now she stiffened and caught hold of her wits.

"Stand up." She tugged the bandage tight and pushed the girl from her lap. "You can stand on your own."

She righted the crying child, who swayed vacantly on her feet. The flies threw themselves against the light above the door, dying and sizzling in acrid smoke.

"Listen to me." Cora spoke warm and low. "Listen. You're not badly hurt. Stop crying. You should go home."

The girl stood without moving.

"Go home. You can't stay here. You can't come here any more."

Now the child turned and looked at her, a bracelet of tears heavy under her lashes.

"Why?"

Coraluna didn't reply immediately. Her heart made stories, told lies, laid excuses.

"Because," she said. "Because you're not my child."

The girl was wide-eyed and almost lidless in the gloom. There had been words without sense, and yet they had weight, like an incantation or a bitter curse. Cora watched her cross the concrete yard, waiting until the white dress was swallowed by the night.

"Mother of God!" Isabel cried when she saw the blood. "What in God's name has happened?"

Cora placed her forehead against the grill, scrutinising the street and its desolation.

"Why didn't you come?"

Isabel waved the spoon she'd carried from the kitchen. "But what happened?" she asked, bewildered.

"Nothing." Cora straightened her torn collar. She swung the wooden frames, snapped the bolts, and closed the shutters on the day.

That evening was the last time Malena came to their home. There was talk later that the family had moved – one of the brothers had qualified as an engineer of some sort, and they'd all moved away to some city. They'd ridden to this life of new luxury, so the story went, in the back of a cattle truck.

Whether the girl left with any sense of injustice or malice, they never knew. Coraluna, who was always practical, believed it to have been for the best.

"She wasn't our child," she said, but Isabel had taken it to heart for the both of them. Their voices scaled the kitchen wall, sliding up in the steam of a rolling boil.

"No one said she was our child! But if she thought of us like family, where was the harm? If I meet Sosa in the street he calls me auntie – but do I know who his mother was? No one does!" She sniffed. "And he's twice my age!"

"It wasn't right to let her think it was true, that we have any ties to her, or she to us."

"And what about her finger? Didn't we owe her something for that? Even if just some comfort, or some milk?"

"What milk? What comfort? Where do we magic up these supplies for strangers? This isn't a hospital."

Isabel slammed the lid on the pot.

"You have an answer for everything except for humanity."

"And all your easy answers are lies." Cora grabbed her sister's arm and pinched it. "What does this have to do with you?

Perhaps you'd feel better if it had been your fault? Yes. You don't want to feel relieved of wrong – you just want to twist and torture yourself. Both of us! You don't mind the accident – no! – you're miserable because you missed the opportunity to be the grandmother. Ha! To be her mother, if you could."

They shoved at each other in the small room, pulling apart and then fighting for grip. A stack of plates fell from the counter, a china cup – fragments exploding under their boots and caught in the weft of their skirts. They waltzed between the chairs, arms locked and grimacing. They fell against the wall and trinkets caught in their plaits and were torn down: pictures in their frames, a row of keys, a small yellow cross. The pot on the stove whistled bone-dry, bouncing its lid in appreciation.

Cora threw her hands at her sister's throat.

"You think things can be anything other than they are now? This is life!" She cast her eyes among the pottery bones, looking for arrowheads and finding only dust. "You, you're fond of taking my life for your own. So take it! You and I are the same! We have nothing else. There can never be anything else now."

They fought with their hands, they reached for eye sockets and delicate skin. They kicked and cursed – and then Isabel reached for the knife.

"As if it were a nothing thing!" she screamed, suddenly unmade from herself. "As if it were a nothing thing that you did!"

She angled the knife with one hand and tried to catch Cora's with the other. They writhed, molten and furious, and then the pot on the stove cracked with all the force of a gun shot.

They glared at each other, panted breath mingling and the words hanging heavy between them.

Isabel unfurled her sister's grip. She straightened the shawl across her shoulders and sat at the table. She proclaimed a single word – "horseshit" – and then stared resolutely at the wall.

The gossamer words were done, the bruises a staccato message that lingered for a few days: a thin veneer on skin, black and mottled fading to yellow, like a sunset in reverse.

~

The fans in the hospital waiting room stirred the dust on warm currents, and scents that pummelled the nostrils: hot tarmac, sweet soda, the thin glaze of disinfectant curling out of the floor.

Isabel pushed along the row of chairs, falling over the hem of her skirt, feeling the sweat in the crease of her back. The younger ones watched her go, but some of the older folk tutted and frowned.

"What's the rush, sister?" one called through his handkerchief. "The doctor won't see you any faster. We've been waiting all day." He put his hand on her arm. "We're all of us dying, you know."

Isabel pushed him away, but by the time she reached the end of the hall the desk was empty – its papers locked in a metal cabinet and the girl gone. The lights in the consultation room beyond had been turned off, the examination table hunkering under a grey shroud. There were other doors, their square windows blind behind gauze and notices. Isabel chose one at random and boldly turned the handle.

It was another waiting room; one more repository of people baking in the slow-cooker evening. Some had curled up across vacant seats, or pulled their shawls over their faces. A young woman slept where she sat at a table, head slumped forward on her arms. An older woman – her mother, maybe – sat folded like a pretzel at her feet.

"Where is everybody?" Isabel asked. "Where are the nurses? The doctors?"

A young man briefly lifted his hat and threw his eyes up at the clock. It had gone 10.

"But there was a girl here – a woman. At this desk. Did you see where she went?"

"The nurses have their own room," he said thickly, and she wondered how far he'd travelled. He nodded his eyes in another direction. "There," he said, and pulled his hat low once more.

The corridors could not be mapped. Right angles led onto identical hallways flanked with glass cabinets of instruments. There were notices about clothing and cleanliness, and rows of doors with their padlocks on show like medallions. Isabel shook her head. This was the new world.

She was somewhere in the bowels of the building. She faltered, and then a voice called after her:

"You can't wait here."

A woman approached her quickly, a frown gouged across her forehead. "Go back to the waiting hall."

And then she was in front of her, this girl they had once known, and it was all so long ago that even a simple greeting sounded foolish in her head. Isabel's mouth fluttered before she could speak.

"It's really you!"

The woman regarded her steadily. "Lady, I don't care if you think I'm the Virgin Mary. You can't wait here. Go back to the main hall." Her voice was deeper now, of course, the vowels mangled and flattened like a man's and all at odds with her dress, her face. A burst of laughter erupted from another room.

"Perhaps you don't remember me –"

"Of course I remember you. We grew up together. We shared a bus every day for five years. Your father knew my father. Our children are in the same district school. And now you want to see a doctor, yes?"

"No. Yes. Of course, or why would we come all this way? My sister is ill. Perhaps you remember my sister? You used to come to our house." It was hard to breathe in the airless corridor. "Not here – in Cecito."

The woman shook her head.

"You have me confused for someone else."

For a moment, it was possible. The woman stood there in her store-bought dress, lined in the face and around the lips. The laughter rang out again and she glanced over her shoulder, the lights catching in her curls.

"You used to come to our house," Isabel said weakly. "You used to make bracelets."

The woman had half-turned and now she stood caught between the laughter and the recollection.

"No … that was you?" She smiled suddenly, and the lines in her face lifted clean away.

"Yes!" Isabel cried. "Well, my sister."

The woman nodded. "Yes, yes," she said, "those bracelets! I remember, but I think – it was so long ago. Your house, the one by the reservoir?"

"The reservoir isn't there any more. It was filled in. We have water tanks now."

"I remember!" Evi said, though the water tanks were long after her time.

They fell silent and regarded each other.

"Coraluna's back there. I came to find you."

"Coraluna?" the woman whispered to the ceiling. "So that's her name!"

"She's back there," Isabel waved her hands agitatedly. "Come."

Evi pressed her fingers against her mouth and shook her head. She wouldn't come. She couldn't. She had paperwork to finish and file; she had to straighten the consultation room before she left. She had to go home – she had children, she had a husband.

"No." She blushed. "I'm sorry about it. Perhaps … perhaps tomorrow."

She was leaving. Her shoes rubbed and squealed against the floor and she was leaving.

"Wait!" Isabel felt her face flush. "I waited all this time to tell you."

"Yes?"

Traffic pulsed and hummed beyond the yellow walls, horns squeezing out a melody that was passed from bus to bus. The noise from the waiting rooms curled along the corridors, a muffled echo of murmuring and disapproval.

"It was an accident." Isabel felt the heat turn liquid beneath the folds of her dress. "That night – the last time we saw each other. I was a foolish old woman, even then. I should have known better. I'm sorry."

"What are you talking about?"

"I'll show you. I'll show you." She grabbed for Evi's hands and stared blindly at the slender fingers tangled among her own – like a musician's, but too smooth, too soft. The wound had been obliterated by time. It had healed, or else had never existed.

"You have me confused for someone else." Evi's lips were twisted in a curious way; she seemed frightened. "I'm sorry about your sister. I can't help you."

Isabel tried to reason with her, but her mouth was sticky and the words unintelligible. She leaned her head against the wall and fought for breath. There was laughter – somewhere – and when she looked round, she was standing in the corridor alone.

The lights in the waiting hall had been dimmed as a courtesy to those who had settled into their chairs for the night. The street had fallen quiet, with just the momentary clatter of a bottle cart being wheeled along the empty road, or watchmen singing the boundaries of the hospital grounds.

At first she couldn't find Coraluna. The rows of drooping heads were all the same shade of grey, the same formless mass. Cora, too, had slumped down in her chair, chin cradled against her chest. Isabel touched her arm lightly and the skin was cool despite the evening's heat.

"So you're back." Cora's voice was muffled, as though crawling from the neck of her dress.

"She wouldn't come."

"I told you."

Isabelle wondered whether the girl would come in the morning as she'd promised. Cora lifted her head a fraction and turned one dark eye towards her.

"Tomorrow, I'm going home."

Isabel nodded. "Yes," she said, "we'll go tomorrow. If Evi will help us we could see a doctor in the morning."

"No. We can't wait here for a doctor to tell us that this is life. Did you think it would last?"

"Ridiculous. You're hardly older than I am."

"Then you too ..." Cora seemed to doze. The clock on the wall counted out the minutes, only to be interrupted by the growl of someone expectorating a wad of phlegm. "Listen. Listen." Her voice faded once more into some approaching dream. "I have money. From all the things I ever made, ever sold. In my brooch box."

"Brooch? What brooch?"

"Do you ever hear me? Money, I said. At the bottom of the wardrobe."

Isabel sank her head into her hands, pressing the jigsaw of skull together lest it fling apart into the four corners of the room.

"Why are you telling me this now? We wasted the whole day waiting here – we could already have seen a doctor!"

"Because. Because I knew you'd do something foolish."

They sat without speaking and, gradually, slept where they sat. In the distance, trucks roared and rushed on, in fearful hurry to some other place.

Isabel woke as the deadbolts were pulled back from the shutters. Beyond them the dawn was hazy, already carrying its load of hot, thick air. Cora's hand had slipped from hers during the night. Realising it she turned beathlessly, only to find another body beside her. Evi had come after all, just as she'd promised. She was sitting next to Coraluna, their heads pressed together, hands entwined as though unravelling secrets, or skeins, or beads.

"You came." Isabel blinked against the new light

Evi regarded her briefly, eyes barely resting on this old woman. "Yes," she said, and turned away.

Isabel willed herself to wake up, or to sleep on. Around her the room was in its various states of rousing: the rustle of paper falling away from cold meat, drawers sliding on their rails, chairs squealing under the desk. Children groggy and curled under chairs and full skirts, grandfathers smoking stoically. Overhead, the fans wound on.

"Is there any news," Isabel asked the shoulder pressed against hers. She lowered her voice. "About a doctor?"

"I just arrived. You'll have to wait. I'll look out some breakfast first." Evi tutted petulantly. "All this way, and they didn't even bring bread." She pushed her way along the row of people just as Isabel had done the night before.

"Oh." She glanced at Isabel without meeting her eyes. "I suppose you'll want to eat, too?"

Isabel shook her head, and fell to staring at the necks in front of her. Something seemed amiss in the morning, and it took her a few moments to realise what it was. She weighed the thought and what it meant, then slid into the vacant chair, her hip warm against her sister's. Cora's hair, Isabel noted, had been combed and piled once more into its unfashionably tight knot.

They turned to regard each other. Cora's mouth was trembling, as though she no longer had strength to be still. Her lips fluttered but her eyes – moving to some distant memory – held an unfamiliar calmness.

"I knew she'd come," Cora said.

Isabel mulled it over, She felt the shape of words in her mouth, felt the weight of them hang heavy and unsaid.

"Yes. We knew."

She held her sister's hand. There seemed nothing more to say.

The Plague House

The kid was sitting on the attic floor, but the way the moonlight drilled through the broken slats it was like riding in the cab of a great freight train. He pursed his lips in the dark and made a chugging noise under his breath. The train picked up speed, the wagons shuffling and rocking behind him like a millipede furrowing into earth.

He leaned back and wiped a hand over his brow. He gulped from an imaginary canteen and paused to watch the countryside rolling by. Somewhere in the world – he knew it must be true – there was sun on yellow fields, and long grass swaying in the wind. There was other children. There was school. There was parents, and TV, and singing along with the words.

The train panted to a stop. The moon hooked itself around the side of the roof and flashed between the rafters. He looked for the face and couldn't find it, and thought maybe it was just a lie that his mother had told him – once.

He tried to fire the engine but the train was gone, and so were the wagons and the sun and the fields. There was only the unlit attic and, somewhere far below, the noise of someone climbing the stairs in stealth.

He wasn't afraid of the dark these days. He knew it for what it was: just the way the world looks when it's sleeping. He slid over to the eaves and peeped into the garden below, at the grass grown thick over an upturned table, like bleached bones poking out of the ground. There were bits of other houses still standing on either side but the boundaries had long collapsed and their gardens grafted into one long wilderness. He looked for flattened turf, for patches that might have told on him.

The footsteps fell silent, causing the boy to glance over his shoulder. At the far end of the attic was a recess in the chimney stack where he slept. It seemed a long way from the cab of the train. He could just make out the pile of clothes on one side, and the white sole of a running shoe peering through the gloom. It didn't matter, he knew, because the fort of tinned food was anyway unmissable, even in the dark. He thought for a moment, curling his fingers through the crack in the roof and into the gutter. He brought the black water to his lips and then frowned, glaring once more into the garden, down there, where he could creep into the long grass and relieve himself.

Somewhere else, in what remained of the house, the footsteps were retreating, retracing the creaks and squeals of the floorboards: down the stairs and onto the porch and away. The kid listened intently, head on one side.

The garden waited, and the house was quiet. He pulled himself across the boards, wondering if he should just go in a corner, and then he wrinkled his nose remembering the way the smells of people – their toilet smells and death stink – had a way of seeping across empty land.

He crawled to the hatch and lay peering into the black mouth of the landing below. He listened again, and again there was nothing. He swung his legs over the edge, and lowered himself into the house.

When the boy came back he was shivering in his T-shirt, Bellamy the dog panting in the creases. He hauled himself into the attic, rolling carefully to avoid the metal pipe lodged in the back of his shirt. He'd found it on the narrow side of the garden, where the grass was taller than he was, where there once had been a shed. He'd run his toe over the debris thoughtfully, hunting for something and not sure what, or why. He'd found a beetle and clapped his hand over it like a tent, then gently half-squashed it and tucked it in his pocket.

Now, sliding forgetfully across the boards, he heard its shell splinter and pop. His hand went to find it – and then he froze. Someone was at the cubby hole, sifting through his wordly belongings. There came a low whistle and a soft, joyless laugh.

"Lawn yubin?" It was a man's voice, gruff and roughened about the edges.

The boy stared at a knothole framed by moonlight and fought the need to touch it. His heart thrummed a melody in the crease of his neck.

The stranger stepped out from behind the chimney, masked by night and almost as silent in his steps.

"Hey. You hear me?"

The kid turned his head away. He knew the words now.

"Easy there." The voice floated nearer. "I knew you was up here is all. I knew you was up here."

The boy rolled to one side, shielding the pipe behind him.

"You just pretended to leave." He spoke steadily, but the accusation was high and unfamiliar in his head.

A boot nuzzled his side, finding the shape of him, and then the stranger crouched down, thick with the rolling aroma of rotten earth.

"You been on your own a while." The stranger sniffed importantly. "Most folk wanna know who you are; that's what they ask first." He squatted there a moment, eyeless in the dark. "I pretended to leave. It's how you flush 'em out."

"Who?"

He felt the man shrug. "Where's your folks at? Dead?"

"No."

"Then?"

"Looking for supplies."

The stranger laughed.

"No one been here for months, mebbe more. 'Cept for some woman down there, in the bedroom. Your ma? Then who?"

No reply.

"You do it?"

"She didn't know I was up here, I heard her." The boy spoke quickly now. "She couldn't walk right. Something got her, maybe dogs." He'd heard them running in the dark; heard their claws skittering over the smooth boards, and the sound of her body falling, then dragged across the floor like a damp rag.

"You're 'bout the only living person in a 50-mile radius."

"There's other people?"

"I seen a commune. Somewhere near the border, but that were months ago. They was talking about starting a farm. I reckon they've eaten each other 'bout now. That what you did to that woman?"

The boy shook his head. The smell of the stranger was suffocating, like being held under a blanket.

"How long you been on your own?"

It was impossible for the boy to know.

"Then what happened to your folks?"

The kid thought carefully. People had started getting sick. Neighbourhoods had emptied and the school was locked up. You couldn't buy cornflakes any more, or bread. More people got sick. Some of them died and others ... well, they just went crazy. Wasn't that it? They went crazy and bad, and they did stuff to other people that they shouldn't of, and that too was part of the sickness because it was like they couldn't stop themselves.

"We left," he said, and talked of a car by the side of the road, keys hanging in the ignition. They'd driven until the engine packed in, and then they walked during the nights, mother and child, just the two of them. They passed rows of houses with the doors torn off. Sometimes you'd see folks still in their clothes but flat-out in the middle of the street. Once there had been a mound of shoes piled up on a corner.

The further they walked, the less they saw. And then there was this street. Everyone that could leave had gone. The boy and his mother had walked around the house, pushing open the doors, stepping softly on the grey carpet.

"I thought we'd sleep in the bedroom but we didn't. Mum said someone might come – someone sick. She made us to stay up here. She said to stay quiet. Not to make a noise. Not to talk. To anyone."

"True." The strange spat into a corner. "But if I was after badness, I'd have done it in the garden when you was pissing."

The kid gave a start, a prickle of fear playing against his spine.

When the man spoke again, he made the words carefully.

"Listen," he said, "I don't even remember the last time I had something from a can. I'm gonna have one of yours. Yeah? I'm just gonna have one of them cans."

The man had a tin opener, a thing which made the boy uneasy.

"You not read? This is dog food." The stranger chewed noisily and swallowed. "But beggars and that. I'd eat the dog."

The kid slid the pipe out of his shirt and pushed it with his finger tips until it just nestled under the eaves. He stretched and sat up with his legs crossed.

After a while the stranger said again, "But your ma's dead. You know that, don't you?"

"Maybe."

"There's no maybe. How long she been gone?"

"Don't know."

"Never thought to go looking?" The fork scraped against the bottom of the tin.

"Mum told me not to."

"And why's that?"

"I don't know! She said to stay here. Don't talk to no one."

The empty tin came rolling across the floor.

"Brought you here to protect you like, and left you. Why? She get sick?"

The boy shook his head invisibly in the dark and the stranger asked again, urgently: "She get sick?"

"No."

"Not sick." The voice had grown languid, as if too tired to articulate the obvious. The man was pacing in a large circle, the kid realised, marking out an arc.

"What name you got?"

"Tom."

"Like hell it is. You know what they call me? Razor-sharp."

The stranger had come up behind him the long way. He heard him now, creaking across the boards and then, suddenly, he was hoisted up by his shirt – toes dangling – and thrust into the moonlight while the stranger eyed him keenly.

He was hanging there a long time. Then the man dropped him and stepped back under the rafters, wiping his hands against his jacket in a whispered refrain.

"You're one of them. You're sick. You're on the turn."

The boy shook his head against the floor. "I'm not!" he cried.

"I never got a look at you before. I didn't know or I'd not come up here. Your kind ... you're carriers. It's in your genes." He spat again, disgusted. "Probably your lot what brought it with you."

"I never come from nowhere. I'm not no kind. I'm like you."

"Infestation!"

"Not me –"

"Parasites! With your dirty blood. Hiding away, breeding like cockroaches, brewing disease. My family? Dead. Wife, son?

Dead. Friends? Turned. And who's left? You. You!" He couldn't speak to go on.

"Something must have happened. Something bad. Maybe she had an accident." The kid's voice caught on imagination. He gulped and stuttered like a candle. "Not me. Maybe she – maybe someone … But not sick. Not her. Not me. Swear."

A bitter voice came back at him, bullet-heavy: "Swear? What promise you making me? Promise my boy'll be OK? Promise you won't kill no one else? Like that woman down there?"

"Not me. Not me."

"Not you? No, not ever again. I'll keep your promise. You won't kill no one else. You won't turn no one else."

"I'm not sick. I swear. I'm not."

The stranger was standing back there in the shadows, like a waiting flood or fury.

"But you will be."

The gap under the eaves, the kid realised, was narrow, but just high enough to slide into. He inched towards it, feeling his way with his free hand.

"Then go," the kid said, the words muffled against his shoulder. "Leave me alone."

There was a moment of silence, and he froze in case the sound of his movement gave him away. Then that voice again like thin butter; greasy with intent and sorrow.

"No can do."

The boy took a chance and shifted his weight closer to the lip of the roof. A few metres more and there was a spot where the boards had rotted away, a porch for the sheer drop to the garden below.

"But why?" He reached for the pipe and couldn't find it. Gone in the black, invisible.

"You're one o' them. It's your nature. You're diseased. You're dirty. You're vermin. Your sickness is inevitable."

The boy was almost inside the ledge when the stranger struck the flint on a lighter. There they were, caught in the glow; ridiculous figures cast in wax. The kid was between the eaves and the attic, mud on his trousers, pockets empty except for stains. The stranger was a tall, lanky fella, face too large for his body – bony, protruding – and his beard like a wire brush caught between chin and chest.

Neither moved, and then both were scrambling. The flame flickered and went out.

Now the stranger had his hand on the kid's leg, dragging him away from the ledge, a thousand splinters piercing his shirt and Bellamy the dog whimpering in the creases. He kicked at the boy, soft boots landing between thin flesh and hard bone. He reached down and rolled him over, pinned his knees against the boy's chest like a pivot and squeezed. The kid was quivering and coughing, thin tears in his eyes and a great blackness around him and inside his head.

"You're dirty," the stranger said and then, in a low poem of desire murmured over and over, "Dirty. Dirty. Dirty."

From the edge of darkness the kid closed his fingers over the pipe, but it was stuck fast in some groove. He retched, breath leaking along with life and catching in his throat. He writhed one last time and the pipe swung clear and through the air, steel meeting bone in a flat note. The stranger's skull was shattered and, as if he didn't even know it, they fought, hands touching in the dark and the boards creaking out the tune of the struggle. Finally the stranger found purchase, wrenching the metal bar into the distance, where it bounced and fell among debris and dun corners.

They lay like that, the boy and the man, shrouded in the dark – a private moment, almost tender. And then the man stood while, far below him, it seemed, the boy retched and grasped at life.

The stranger muttered as he stood, rocking and swaying as though praying in a foreign tongue.

"You're dirty," he said. "Diseased." He fell silent, mulling something over. After a while he said, "Maybe it's better this way. Everything you touch you turn black."

He was slurring, running the words down the front of his shirt. He took a step and halted, then stepped once more – a tentative kind of waltz. He slouched and then tipped forward in a fluid movement, knees buckled up behind him. He yelped as he went down, and then laughed softly to himself.

"Been watching you," he said. "Been watching a while." He clawed his hands acrpss the floor, head heavy as mercury and just as viscous. "You want to know why she didn't come back? Your mum?"

The kid stiffened, catching a coughing fit and holding it in his throat.

"Why?"

The stranger swallowed laboriously.

"She dint want you. She dint want you. She ..." He trailed off, as though fetching a long-distant memory, or had fallen asleep where he lay. "She dint care about you. Said you was a bastard, said you wasn't even hers."

The boy knew it as a lie, the kind that had parents told – once. He stuffed his hands against his ears.

"I saw her one time in her dress. Dirty, ragged thing. Desperate for a man, she was. Gagging. Me and my boys, we had her. You hear me? All of us. And you know – d'you know?" The voice faded into the woodwork and the patina of dust.

The kid tried to block the words out. The ones he heard were only half known, but he felt them all the same.

"Afterwards, she said thank you." The stranger touched the dent in his head against the floorboards. He tried to spit, and couldn't. He was breathing slow and heavy, a locomotive lullaby, and then that too stopped.

The boy held back the burn in his throat. He'd heard the creak of timbers and knew the man lay still now, somewhere near the hatch. He wondered if once more it was a lie.

The sky was shifting, turning in its colours from black to blue. Now he could just see the shape of the stranger lumpen against the floor and then, as he watched, heard a snake-like hiss, a crescendo that grew faster as it grew louder. The kid stumbled forward too late; too late to catch the body as it slid and fell through the hatch face-first and onto the landing below. The sound of it: it was like the weight of the world, crashing down and immediately silenced.

The boy sat against the curve of the roof, barefoot as the day he was born, and thought about dead life and dead times. He sat too long, and when it was too late he crawled to the hatch and peered down at the damp rag of the man below, more visible now in the breaking day. The stranger had landed on his side, one hand impossible behind him and turned the wrong way.

It was a foolish regret, the boy knew, because the weight of the stranger had been immovable against his chest. And now he was lying there, a heavy beacon to bring dogs, or others – and that just couldn't be.

The kid sat a while longer, and then he crawled to his belongings, once more searching for something: some tool, some salvation.

He worked quickly, pawing though his things and then, with something clasped in his fist, retraced his steps to the attic door, jumping the tracks and climbing nimbly between the rafters.

The sky through the broken eaves was pale and full of empty, eternal promise. From the edge of the universe – in some other world – the sun came up.

No, the kid knew. It just couldn't be like this.

He swung his legs over the hatch and lowered himself into the house. He whistled as he set to his task, to keep away the feeling, but gradually the sound died away and day was still. He no longer remembered the tune.

Of Icarus

It was a warm, wet breeze which drifted through the farm that day. It set the leaves trembling and spinning to the ground, and when the birds called out their chirruping was thrown and lost among the deadfall. The wind shook the ripples from the face of the stream. It crept around the side of the barn and it settled among the fallow grass – among roots and dank soil – and waited.

It was a thing which hadn't been seen in those parts – at least, not for some time: the way the clouds rushed on and the sun stippled the land without promise of heat, and the watchful manner of cows at cud, and all of nature coiled as if the day itself were paused.

The man known as Hill had grown old alone, and had that look of solitude – which is to say unkempt, but unconcerned by it. He was caught between two worlds – of living and loneliness – and mostly was to be found in heavy boots, and mealy mouthed. Now he leaned against a wall and watched the long grass churned in pinwheels, as though the world was shook, or he were, and it was impossible to know which the wind moved first.

This was in the weeks following a fire in the barn; a blaze which had toasted the rafters and left the roof sagging in a drunken leer. He'd had Crawford come out to look it over – the blue van was still hitched up on the dirt track – but all thoughts of supervising had been sucked clear of the day. The afternoon was airless and yet the grass swayed, rushing on itself in perfect circles: twin-engine spirals that shushed and hummed across the field, racing back and forth like a semaphore.

Crawford came around the side of the house wiping his neck with a rag. "I'll be off," he said, and waited.

Hill tipped his head at the grass: "You seen the like of it?"

Crawford looked into the field and at the lip of oaks gathered along its far edge. He saw the row of water butts angled on their props like squat-bellied scarecrows, and paper scraps lying sodden in the beck. "Naw," he agreed. "I'll be off, then?"

Hill spared him a glance. "The wind. You seen the wind?"

Crawford wiped his hands and said not lately. He grinned to himself, all the while reckoning up what there'd be for dinner.

The old man turned to face him. He squinted into the low sun and rattled the wooden chimes on their strings.

"You see this, smart fella? Wind chime. No wind, no chime."

Crawford wasn't one to take any feeling in excess. He took a sideways glance at the older man, sizing him up since last he'd seen him. Hill was brewing girth beneath his jacket, and that was unusual for a labouring man. He seemed looser in the face, and more wrinkled, but then he'd always had that weathered aspect. He was watery in the eyes, though, and the sun had burnished him bright, burst capillaries across the nose and cheeks. Maybe he was a drinking man, Crawford speculated. Maybe he was a drinking man and he'd had himself a little nip at back of the barn and here he was, swaying and surly and a king of all the world.

"Right," Crawford laughed. "No wind."

"Then what's that?" Hill asked, and turned to gaze once more over the fallow field, where the grass turned on of its own accord.

The stalks were coming on for a foot and a half, fat and proud in the base and tapering to needle points. From where they watched it was liquid motion; green light that spun on itself and rebounded to each corner of the meadow in turn.

Crawford scratched his cheek. "Aw, heck," he said, "that's not wind. That's vermin. See how it moves from the bottom up?" He trailed off, foolish for telling a man like Hill how grass grows.

"It's not moles nor rats."

"No? What d'you make of it, then?"

"I seen it before," Hill said. "Once. Long time ago."

The yard beside the house was silent. It had its collection of machinery: the teeth of a plough rusting away without a word, tyres dropped where they'd rolled. It was a wasting world, barren and so alone that even the wind had left it be. Crawford wondered if he should invite Hill to come eat at his place, then baulked at the thought of asking a man that even the world couldn't touch.

"Yeah?" he asked instead, "when was that?"

"Before your time." Hill raised a hand halfway up his chest. "I was a kid."

"Give over. You?"

"Aye. I seen this then. I ain't a superstitious man, but a wind like this brings happenings."

"Give over, old man! You'll be getting your wijji board out next."

"What you getting antsy 'bout? I didn't say it was bad happenings. It's an ill wind that blows no good." Hill's eyes drifted up to the cloudless sky. "But sometimes it blows things you'll never see not more'n once, twice, in your life – if you're lucky. Keep your eyes open, fella. Wide open."

There was empty pasture as far as the horizon. Smoke curled up from a chemical plant lodged somewhere out west, the tendril reaching straight up like a pale grey cord. Crawford squinted for the nearest town and found nothing. Ain't that the view from nowhere, he thought, and here was Hill with his yabber on all of a sudden. He glanced up as the old man had done, watching evening come on in the distance like a late Spring bloom.

"Aw, heck," he said. "What did you see?"

"Days like this'n. Windless days. Nothing moving. Everything slow and lazy; even the water slowed down. It was like there was no flow to nothing. Cows was the same back then, too – wary for something. You'd be advised to leave 'em be, days like this."

Crawford fished a smoke from his pocket, cradling the spilled tobacco in his palm. "Oh, for sure," he said, with no hint of a smile, "for sure."

"Few days after that first windless day, the water really did stop. And I don't mean it wasn't coming out the pipes. As I heard it, Leder Falls just stopped, stock still, right in the act of flowing. You could put your hands to it and bring 'em out wet as you like, but the water was just hanging there. Not going up, not coming down."

"Yeah?" Crawford exhaled a jet of smoke. "You see it?"

Hill shrugged. "I heard it is all."

Crawford turned away from the blade-edged afternoon. "Whyn't you come eat with us this evening? You'd have an audience. I know Lena would want to hear this an' all."

"No." The older man chewed on his cheek and added that he was grateful.

Crawford zipped his jacket with a flourish. "Got that quote to give you," he said, but when he found the square of paper he stood tapping it in his hand. "So I should keep my open for frozen waterfalls, you saying?"

Hill's eyes caught the low sun and glinted, catlike.

"Naw. The waterfall was just one thing we heard about – we all heard about it in these parts. You just ask your folks. Well, your dad. He'll know it."

"I'll ask him. But it's funny he never mentioned it before. This place must have been crawling with journalists. A thing like that stays talked about. It's a wonder I ain't heard of it."

Hill appraised him up and down. "It was over before it started. There was no time to call out your busy bodies. It was just something we heard from a few folk was there at the time. Thing is, what happened at Leder, it was a sign."

"Sign of what?"

Hill turned to face him. "People flew."

Up close Hill smelled of damp down; a thick, pungent odour. Crawford wondered if the other man was even aware of it any more, or of the seam slowly laddering along his shoulder.

"Flew? Where to?"

Hill jerked his thumb straight up.

"Yeah?" Crawford felt vaguely uneasy, later reasoning it was because he'd never been much for religious sentiment. "They disappeared?"

"Naw. Naw, you dim wit. Ain't talking 'bout that. I mean they just straight-up flew. Not into outer space. Twenty, thirty feet. Like they'd sprouted wings and just took off, stayed up for an hour and then they floated right back down again." His face took on a queer expression. "Musta been something, alright. And you know the thing of it is?" He waited until Crawford shook his head. "It was just kids. No one else, just kids, and only some of 'em. Straight up: they flew and came back."

"What, like angels?"

"What's wrong with you? You got Bible on the brain? They didn't have wings. They just lifted up off the ground, clean off their feet, like the wind just picked 'em up and carried 'em straight up. And when they came down, it was so gentle like."

Crawford watched his face closely. Hill's voice had taken on a soft lilt, as though those children had landed so gracefully that he daren't imprint the memory of it with any kind of force. He played it over in his mind afterwards, seeing Hill's heavy features soften like he was talking to a kitten.

"But it was just kids, and just some of 'em. Those that was there kept it to themselves for the most part, and those that didn't – well, no one believed 'em.

"There was one kid, though – Swann's boy – he took off and raced the clouds. As if he could! Came down on the lake and was pulled under and nivver came back up. That's in one of your newspapers. But they just said he drowned. I suppose he did."

"And you were there? You … flew?"

Hill shoved his fists into his coat pockets, and the frayed seam gave way with a tut.

"This was back in '62. I was badly; swollen up fatter than a hamster. Couldn't see no one, couldn't go nowhere; like that. It was Wiley what told me. Come up in the bedroom with his spotty face all red, jumping about. Couldn't speak for trying.

"Wiley was there when it happened. Group of five, six of 'em, out by the marshes. Suzy Tanner was there. Floated up like a silk balloon, Wiley said. Straight up in her dress." Hill whistled, eyes fixed a hundred miles away or more.

"Wiley? Jo Wiley was one of the kids that flew?"

"Suzy Tanner got married, you know. Well, course she did. Lives in Norway now." Hill looked incredulous, as though of all things, this was the unbelievable fact.

"I know the Wiley lot. Old Jo Wiley flew?"

Hill shook his head impatiently.

"No, not him neither. Unlucky, the pair of us. Wind never took him no place – don't know why. And later, he got sick, didn't he? Got some kind of brain fever. Poor bastard."

Crawford jiggled in his boots. "So you didn't fly. Wiley didn't fly. Suzy Tanner flew, but she's in Norway now. I don't know, Jack."

"What you got that you know? Nothing. That's why I'm telling you. You know what Wiley told me? Said it was his greatest regret. Said he watched Suzy Tanner float up, Bob Thornton, that weedy one – something Mills, always a sour face on him. They took off like kites, but Wiley was grounded like a sack of sugar. Tried to take off himself: jumped off rocks, almost broke his neck. Me too, later. You know what that was like? Stuck in bed and Wiley telling you this thing – even to have seen it, that'd been something. I tell you, it'd be something."

"Don't you wonder ..." Crawford shrugged expansively.

"What?"

"Well ... whether it was true."

The clear sky was growing to purple overhead, sun hunting low on the horizon. Hill waited a full minute before speaking, his face as gnarled as the oaks in the distance.

"Why wouldn't it be?"

"Cos they was kids."

Hill considered it. "Dint you ever know when your luck was in? Like, itchy fingers, and then your cards come up? Or there's a storm 'bout to break, and you smell it – smell th'electricity? It was like that then. I knew something was up even before Wiley told me; I just couldn't do nothing about it.

"You know how long I lived with that? Like waking up and wanting to run – run until your lungs burst and you're burning all over – only someone says 'no, boy – you wait.' And you wait, and you wait, like counting off a clock for 50 years. What you know about that, son?"

They turned and watched a bee crawling on the ground, fat in its fur and dopey as hell, staggering along the cracks in the ground. Hill squatted down with a grunt and let the bee climb into his hand. He brought it up to his face and scrutinised it, as though it was a rare and marvellous creation. For the second time, Crawford wondered if Hill had been drinking.

"No," Crawford said slowly. "I don't know about that. But it seems strange to me, is all."

"Damn right," Hill told the bee.

Crawford hesitated. "Not about the flying. I mean ... regretting something that weren't yours to regret."

Hill was still – very still. And then his low-down voice crawled into the afternoon: "No? Why's that?"

Crawford cast a desperate glance at the van. He was in over his head.

"If it happened, it was Wiley who was there that day. If it didn't, what difference does it make? But you tell it as though you was there, and you hold on to it like you missed out on something. But I ... I just don't see it."

Hill breathed across the back of the bee and it lit up and took off, wings working furiously, wobbling and wavering just a few inches above ground. When it reached the edge of the field it accelerated sharply and was pulled away and out of sight, just a small black speck vanished by the grass.

The world was two men leaning against the barn with their hands in their pockets and nothing left to say. They stood without moving, and only their shadows shifted against the brickwork.

"Well, I'll be off, then." Crawford slid the square of paper towards Hill. "You change your mind we eat at 7, around then."

That was all that was said, Crawford would say later; that was the sum of the afternoon. By the time he got back in the van the old man had gone back to crouching low against the ground. Crawford shook his head and tried to laugh it off, but there was something sour about the evening; as though something distasteful had occurred but the thing of it was a secret. He turned the van down the dirt track, bouncing over pot holes. His last glimpse of Hill in the mirror juddered and broke free, the image of the man sliding away between hedges rows and the blank sky.

Once Crawford had gone there was no one left but Hill. The cows, growing restless, lined themselves up along the fence in perfect order of some kind. They rested their heads on the poles and watched him, blinking slow and steady.

Hill stayed a while, as though the wind had blown through him and carried away some vital part. The afternoon dropped down through its scale of residual heat and the chill set in. He glanced back at the cows. He must have been reckoning something or other, because he nodded at them. And then he went inside the house and closed the door on their regard.

He tugged his jacket off and hung it in the hall. He circled the living room, running his hands over the backs of the chairs. He picked up a photo and looked briefly into it. He placed it on the edge of the table, and in everything he did, moved with gentleness. He climbed the stairs and the loose wood groaned and cried out and he let it, playing the timbers like a tune, as though all the years were condensed into those noises.

Upstairs it was still light at the windows, the dust rising up to meet him. He took his shirt off and laid it carefully on the bed. He saw himself do it in the mirror and watched in fascination. The way his flesh hung down, the hairs sprouting of their own accord – it was none of it familiar.

He pulled the suitcase out from under the bed and smoothed the grit from its lid. He felt its buckles, and how they'd last forever. The suitcase had never been more than 50, maybe 100 miles from that room, as though it had lived its life on an elastic string.

Inside, curling and frayed, was a harness – a broad frame of leather with loops for his arms and a belt to place around his chest. Hanging in symmetry from the frame were wings – not like angels wings, no: they'd been moulded of light plastic and pegged over with taut rubber and small, hollow tubes, like a kite. He shook it out and held it against himself, watching once more in the mirror and marvelling at the way his body smoothed behind the material.

Suddenly, he was doubtful. He sat on the bed, the wings buckling against his lap. He played his fingers against the wool of the bedspread; over the nubs and bumps of the roses that someone, once, had stitched along its border.

He slid his arms into the contraption and tightened the fasteners. At first the wings drooped sadly behind him, like a shawl, and then he pulled the straps tight and shook himself, and they rose proud and sleek behind him.

Sun was low, shadows edging across the floorboards and peeking under the bed. Hill stepped to the window and threw the shutters out into the sky. He climbed onto the sill and stood there awkwardly, surveying the world. The wind had returned on a soft breath, and it seeped into the room and along his bare skin. Dusk curled along the horizon. The evening seemed salted and bitter – somewhere, there was a storm coming on but below, the grass danced on. Hill eased himself past the shutters. He hesitated – just for a moment – and then he stepped among the clouds, and flew.